# SPIRIT SLEUTHS

## HOW MAGICIANS AND DETECTIVES EXPOSED THE GHOST HOAXES

### GAIL JARROW

WINNER OF THE YALSA AWARD FOR EXCELLENCE
IN NONFICTION FOR YOUNG ADULTS

CALKINS CREEK
AN IMPRINT OF ASTRA BOOKS FOR YOUNG READERS
New York

For information about permission to reproduce selections from this book,
please contact permissions@astrapublishinghouse.com.

Calkins Creek
An imprint of Astra Books for Young Readers, a division of Astra Publishing House
astrapublishinghouse.com
Printed in Malaysia

ISBN: 978-1-6626-8023-6 (hc)
ISBN: 978-1-6626-8024-3 (eBook)

Library of Congress Cataloging-in-Publication Data

Names: Jarrow, Gail, author.
Title: Spirit sleuths : how magicians and detectives exposed the ghost
    hoaxes / Gail Jarrow.
Description: First edition. | New York : Calkins Creek, 2024. | Includes
    bibliographical references. | Audience: Ages 10-17 | Audience: Grades
    5-12 | Summary: "After millions of people died during World War I and
    from the 1918 influenza pandemic, the popularity of spiritualism soared.
    Desperate to communicate with their dead loved ones, the bereaved fell
    prey to extortion by fraudulent mediums and fortune tellers. But
    magician Harry Houdini wasn't fooled. He recognized the scammers'
    methods as no more than conjurer tricks. Angered by the way people were
    exploited, Houdini set out to expose the ghost hoaxes. In his stage
    show, he revealed the fraudsters' techniques, and he used a team of
    undercover investigators to collect proof of séance deceptions. His
    head secret agent was a young New York private detective and disguise
    expert, Rose Mackenberg-a woman who continued her ghost-busting career
    for decades, long after Houdini's death in 1926"-- Provided by
    publisher.
Identifiers: LCCN 2023045804 (print) | LCCN 2023045805 (ebook) | ISBN
    9781662680236 (hardcover) | ISBN 9781662680243 (ebk)
Subjects: LCSH: Houdini, Harry, 1874-1926--Juvenile literature. |
    Mackenberg, Rose., 1892-1968--Juvenile literature. | Impostors and
    imposture--United States--History--20th century--Juvenile literature. |
    Mediums--United States--History--20th century--Juvenile literature. |
    Magicians--United States--History--20th century--Juvenile literature. |
    Spiritualism--United States--History--20th century--Juvenile literature.
Classification: LCC GV1545.H8 J37 2024  (print) | LCC GV1545.H8  (ebook) |
    DDC 793.8092 [B]--dc23/eng/202311-06
LC record available at https://lccn.loc.gov/2023045804
LC ebook record available at https://lccn.loc.gov/2023045805

First edition
10 9 8 7 6 5 4 3 2 1

Design by Barbara Grzeslo
The text is set in Sabon LT Std.
The titles are set in Baliey Sans ITC Std; A-heads are set in Mader Regular.

For Elgin Booker—May you always find life's magic

# CONTENTS

# CHAPTER ONE
# A VISIT WITH GHOSTS

*"I there witnessed physical manifestations which demonstrated to me beyond all doubt that they were not produced by mortal hands."*
—*Judge J. W. Edmonds, 1853*

The room feels spooky as soon as you walk in.

Heavy maroon curtains cover the windows. The carpet muffles your footsteps. You catch a whiff of incense.

Your host invites you to sit with her at a round mahogany table along with eight other visitors. She tells everyone in the circle to join hands.

The lights are turned off. You can see nothing. A bell jingles, first on one side of the room, then the other, and finally near your head.

You hear knocks on the wooden table. Your host announces that the spirits have arrived. "Does anyone have a question for them?" she says.

The man to your left asks whether his friend is happy in the spirit world.

Two knocks.

"The spirits reply 'yes,'" the host explains.

Several people in the circle inquire about a dead relative, their money troubles, or their love life. Each time, the ghosts answer with knocks.

Tiny lights flicker above the table and dart around the room. A tambourine rattles in the blackness.

Suddenly, the table rises, tilts to the side, then thuds back to the floor. The next moment, you feel your chair rise, too. For a few seconds, you're floating.

A glistening white hand appears a few feet away. You feel your hair being pulled. Something clammy touches your cheek. A chill runs down your spine.

Above the table, a shining horn appears in the darkness. It turns toward the woman across from you, and an eerie voice comes from the trumpet. "Your daughter is with you," it murmurs. The woman sobs.

Then you notice a shimmery white form in a corner of the room. It's the size and shape of a man, and he has a face. When the woman next to you screams, the figure instantly vanishes.

Have you just seen a ghost? Have you heard a spirit talk?

Nearly 175 years ago, scientists, magicians, journalists, and detectives began investigating whether ghosts existed. Many people condemned them for asking the question. Others tried to keep the truth hidden. That didn't stop the spirit sleuths.

Their search for answers required quick wits, ingenuity, and pluck. What they discovered was shocking and surprising. But was it supernatural?

This is their story.

A ghostly photograph
from 1899

8

## CHAPTER TWO

# SPEAKING TO THE DEAD

"They came . . . proclaiming the joyful tidings that
they all 'still lived.'"
—*Emma Hardinge, 1870*

It all started in March 1848 with two brown-haired girls in a
farmhouse bedroom.

The exact details of the event depended on who was telling
the story, and when. But according to one widely shared version,
Margaretta Fox (also called Maggie or Margaret) was fourteen
and her younger sister, Catharine (later known as Katie or Kate),
had just turned eleven.

About four months before, the Fox family had temporarily
moved into the house in the upstate New York community of
Hydesville while they were building a new home nearby. In
early March, the girls' mother began hearing odd knocking and
thumping noises during the night. At first, she thought it was
furniture being moved or footsteps on the wooden floor. But after
she lit a candle and checked the house, Mrs. Fox saw that
everything was in its place.

On Friday, March 31, 1848 (the night before April Fools'
Day), the sisters announced that they heard noises every evening
at bedtime. They told their parents that it sounded as if someone
was tapping a foot on the floor or knocking on doors.

The girls claimed that they had developed a code of raps for communicating with the source of the mysterious sounds. They called the knocker Mr. Splitfoot, another name for the devil. Using raps, he answered yes or no questions. Two raps for yes. Silence for no.

Their mother was convinced that ghosts were making the noises. She asked Splitfoot, "Is this a human being that answers my questions so correctly?"

No rap.

"Is it a spirit? If it is, make two raps," she went on.

The Fox farmhouse, where spiritualism is said to have begun. The sign above the door reads "SPIRITUALISM originated MAR 31st 1848 IN THIS HOUSE." Around 1916, the house was moved from Hydesville to Lily Dale, New York, a spiritualist community 150 miles (241 km) away. The building burned down in 1955.

Two of the Fox sisters in an 1852 photograph.
Margaretta (1833–1893) (left), known as Maggie or Margaret, claimed to have married Elisha Kane, an Arctic explorer who later died in 1857. She used his name, but his family denied that the marriage ever took place.
Catharine (1837–1892), known as Katie or Kate, married a British lawyer and spiritualist named Henry Jencken with whom she had two sons. He died in 1881.

Two loud raps.

Mrs. Fox had heard a rumor that a man was killed in the house. By asking the spirit more questions, she and the girls learned that he had been a thirty-one-year-old peddler. The ghost confirmed with knocks that he'd been robbed and murdered in the house and that his body was buried in the basement.

Mrs. Fox invited her neighbors to witness the knocking themselves. The spirit was able to answer questions about their families, such as how old their children were. The neighbors were as amazed as Mrs. Fox.

Reports of ghostly rappings in Hydesville quickly circulated in the area. Dozens of curious local people visited the farmhouse. A group of them dug up the dirt basement floor in search of the peddler's body. But instead of finding bones, they hit groundwater and had to stop digging as the floor flooded.

## ROCHESTER RAPPING

Unnerved by the presence of a ghost, the girls' parents moved out of the haunted farmhouse. They sent Maggie and Katie to live with their adult sister Leah Fox Fish, a piano teacher in Rochester about 30 miles (48 km) away.

The knocking followed the girls.

Leah spread the word in Rochester about her younger sisters and the mysterious rappings. The news lit a fire in central New York.

Rochester was a thriving city on the shore of Lake Ontario in the Finger Lakes section of the state. Many of the region's well-educated residents were open to unconventional ideas, and the area had become a breeding ground for reforms in politics and religion.

Some people were active in movements to abolish slavery and to give women the right to vote. The first Seneca Falls Women's Rights Convention would be held in July 1848, about 25 miles (40 km) from the Fox house in Hydesville.

Others had adopted religious viewpoints that differed from the teachings of the traditional Protestant and Catholic churches in the United States. These included the belief that the sick could be cured through magnetic power transmitted by someone laying hands on their bodies. Another idea was that spirits of the dead existed in an afterlife and could speak to a living person who was in a trance.

The concept of life after an earthly death had been part of many cultures and religions for thousands of years. Tales of ghostly knocking and rattling had been told for centuries. Still, the story of the Fox sisters and Splitfoot's rappings grabbed the attention of central New Yorkers in an unprecedented way.

The idea that spirits could communicate with the living was appealing. During the 1840s—a time before vaccines, antibiotics, and other effective medicines—disease often tragically and prematurely ended lives. People were drawn to the notion that the body's death was merely a spirit's birth into the next stage. They embraced the thought that the ghost of a loved one was still close by, watching and helping them through their daily struggles. What a comfort to know that death was not the end and that it was possible to talk with those who had passed away!

When these believers heard about Maggie and Katie Fox, they considered the knocking communication to be proof that the human spirit survives beyond death. The spiritualists, as they named themselves, were convinced that individuals like the Fox girls had a special ability to receive and convey messages from the spirit world. These gifted people were called "mediums."

The sisters became a sensation.

## SPOOKY SÉANCES

By now, more spirits had joined Splitfoot in communicating through Maggie and Katie. In addition to the yes or no responses, the ghosts spelled out answers to questions using the alphabet. When someone called out or pointed to the correct written letter, the spirit knocked three times.

According to Leah, the spirits directed her to promote her sisters. She organized private séances with Maggie and Katie so that the public had a chance to communicate with the spirits. Leah asserted that she had the same power as her younger sisters to beckon the spirits, and she held séances of her own.

A séance was usually set up in a darkened room with a table in the middle. The lights were turned down because the spiritualists said that strong light disturbed the ghosts.

Spiritualism.—Mrs. ANN LEAH BROWN (of the Fox Family) is still at home, No. 1 Ludlow-place, corner of Houston and Sullivan-sts., where persons may, on her usual terms, avail themselves of her peculiar powers as a Spirit Medium. Hours—From 3 to 5 and from 7 to 10 p. m.

Ann Leah (about 1813–1890), known as Leah, was married three times and went by a succession of last names: Fish, Brown, Underhill. She paid for this advertisement in the *New-York Daily Tribune*, December 30, 1856, in which she offers "her peculiar powers as a Spirit Medium." Mediums have advertised their services ever since.

Visitors, called sitters, sat in a circle around the table with the girls. One of the Foxes requested that the spirits make themselves known. The group heard tapping. As a sitter asked a question, a ghost knocked in reply.

Often sitters wanted to know if a loved one was at peace and still nearby. Others asked about the future of their romantic life, career, finances, or health. When the spirit answered certain questions correctly (such as "How old was my sister when she died?" or "How many children do I have?"), the visitors were awestruck.

In November 1849, Leah and Maggie presented their first large demonstration of spirit rapping in a Rochester auditorium. Hundreds of people paid a quarter (equal to about $10 today) to see the sisters receiving messages from the dead in response to questions from the audience.

As their popularity grew, Leah took Maggie and Katie on

tour throughout New York State. The sisters were nicknamed the Rochester Knockers, or the Ghost Seers. In New York City, crowds paid a dollar a person (nearly $40 today) to attend a demonstration of the ghost communication.

To their audiences, Maggie and Katie seemed too young and innocent to be anything other than authentic mediums. They clearly had special power. Soon the Fox sisters were collecting thousands of dollars from their appearances.

In 1850, a reporter attended one of the Fox sisters' private afternoon séances at a New York City hotel. Writing for the *New-York Daily Tribune*, he described Maggie and Katie as teens with dark eyes and hair and "complexions of transparent paleness."

The three sisters sat on a sofa behind a table. The reporter and his friend took seats across from them. Immediately, the men heard loud rapping on the table and on the wooden floor. Leah explained that this meant the spirits were willing to talk to the visitors.

The reporter thought about a person who had died years before and asked, "Are you a relative?"

He heard and felt two thumps on the floor near his feet. Yes.

"How many years since you were living?"

Twenty-seven knocks.

These answers fit the individual in his mind.

Throughout the questioning, the reporter heard raps that sounded different and came from other parts of the room. The Foxes said there were five spirits present, and they were also sending messages. One was a child whose faint table knocks were hard to hear.

Although most of the reporter's additional questions were answered correctly, only one of his friend's six questions were. At that point, the spirits refused to participate anymore that afternoon.

The *Tribune* reporter wrote that he never saw any of the Foxes move in a way that could create the tapping. The girls seemed so sincere, he said, that it was hard to conclude that they were deceiving their visitors. Yet he was "not willing to believe that spirits have nothing better to do than make fruitless revelations by means of thumps and raps."

16

## TIPPING TABLES

As the Fox sisters became known far from New York, spiritualism grew at an astounding pace. Many educated and prominent people from the fields of literature, politics, and science became interested in the new religion. "We found our so-called *dead* were all living," wrote one early spiritualist.

Thousands of Americans were convinced that spirits could contact the living. Even those who regularly attended traditional church services embraced the ability to connect with the spirit world.

The most devout spiritualists established rituals for séances that involved singing hymns and reading Christian religious tracts. They published pamphlets and articles to educate the public on the way to conduct a séance. People formed private circles of friends and family to communicate with the spirit world and to study spiritualism.

One enthusiastic follower, who was a New York State judge, praised spiritualism because it "comforts the mourner and binds up the broken-hearted" and "smooths the passage to the grave and robs death of its terrors."

By 1850, just two years after the first rappings in the bedroom of Maggie and Katie Fox, hundreds of people—men, women, even children—announced that they also had the power to contact spirits during a séance.

Many spiritualists considered females more sensitive to the spirit world, just as the Fox sisters were. In one description of a séance, the medium was described as "a young, innocent girl of some fifteen" who would not deceive the group.

While mediums often held private sittings, others performed to large crowds in theaters and lecture halls, charging for their appearances.

As the number of mediums increased, the spirits made their presence known in new ways. During séances, the table rose from the floor before shaking and tilting. Visitors suddenly heard eerie music from drums and horns. In the dark, a glowing trumpet materialized in midair. The spirits used it to amplify their voices as they spoke to the sitters.

Some mediums seemed to fall into a trance during a séance. The spirits answered questions by speaking through the medium's mouth or by using the medium's hand to write.

Séance visitors were transfixed by these powerful experiences. Receiving a message from a dead relative was an emotional moment. One man attended an 1852 séance at which he believed the spirit of his nephew had communicated with him. "Mourn no more for the loss [of] a dear soul—" the man wrote in a letter, "he lives! he lives! in a Glorious world of light & love."

By 1850, newspaper stories about the Foxes and their "Spirit Knockings" appeared throughout the US. Headlines from: the *Davenport* [IA] *Gazette*, August 15, 1850; *Richmond* [IN] *Palladium*, February 20, 1850; *Minnesota Pioneer*, August 22, 1850.

## GENUINE OR FAKE?

Protestant and Catholic church leaders dismissed this new religious movement. They declared that spirit communication was a sign of evil akin to witchcraft.

And not everyone was sure that the Rochester Knockers were actually calling forth the spirits of the dead. Several doctors who had observed the Foxes' demonstrations argued that Maggie and Katie—not ghosts—produced the raps by cracking their knee and foot joints beneath their long skirts. The sound resonated through hard surfaces like a wooden floor.

Leah agreed to let the physicians perform tests during which the girls' knees were held and their feet placed on cushions. But without physically examining the girls more carefully, which

Leah wouldn't allow, the doctors lacked strong proof of their hypothesis.

To the Fox sisters' spiritualist supporters, no amount of testing and examining could ever prove that the Foxes were anything but true mediums.

The press was generally skeptical of spiritualism. In 1851, a journalist named C. Chauncey Burr gave speeches in New York City and around the country during which he described the raps as "pretended answers from the spiritual world." As part of these lectures, Burr's friend demonstrated that the "Spiritual Knockings" were far from ghostly by creating his own rapping sounds.

One New York newspaper commented on the rappings: "No rational mind believes that the spirits of another world have anything to do with them; but their cause has as yet, so far as we know, not been fully explained."

A Philadelphia column read: "It is most surprising, however, that their [the spirits'] means of communication with mortals are narrowed down to the simple faculty of knocking. One would think that it would be as easy for ghosts to utter articulate words as to knock on chairs and tables."

Newspapers printed stories about people who had been duped and cheated out of their money by self-proclaimed mediums. In one case, a medium convinced a grieving New York farmer to hand over $13,000 (about $465,000 today) based on messages from his dead brother and daughter.

Despite the bad press, spiritualism captivated the public. By 1853, tens of thousands of Americans were followers. Spiritualism had spread to other countries, too. Dozens of newspapers, magazines, and books were dedicated to the religious movement.

Séances and medium demonstrations became increasingly popular. The people who attended weren't all believers in spiritualism. Some were curious or wanted to be amused. In the nineteenth century—long before radio, recorded music, television, movies, or computers—the public turned to live performances such as lectures and stage plays for entertainment. Séances joined the list of options.

Magicians took notice.

# HOW DID THEY DO IT?

## TABLE TIPPING

During some séances, the table rose from the floor, then tilted or moved sideways. The medium told sitters that spirits caused the motion.

Fake mediums had several ways of moving tables. Their tricks were easily concealed in the darkness of the séance room. Often the table appeared heavier than it actually was.

In one method, an assistant pushed a pole through a hole in the floor under the table. Using it, he could levitate the table and produce raps.

In another technique, the medium's assistant posed as a customer. The two sat across from each other at the table. Before the séance, they each attached strong metal hooks or rods to wrist bands hidden by their sleeves. On a signal, they both slid the metal under the table edge and lifted. Their hands stayed flat on the tabletop, and the sitters never realized what was going on. If the séance table was light enough, this trick worked with table knives slipped up the sleeves.

## RAPPINGS

While skeptics suspected the Fox sisters of cracking their joints to produce the ghostly knocking, fake mediums had many other methods. When the lights were off, the medium's actions were hidden. In the dark, it's difficult to locate the source of a sound, and sitters believed the taps came from wherever the medium suggested.

In one trick, the medium kept his thumbs close together on top of the table and clicked the fingernails together. The clicks resonated through the wooden table, sounding like raps.

Some fake mediums tapped the leg of the séance table with their shoe heel or knee. Others concealed a clicker in the palm of their hand.

Another method involved the hollow heel of a shoe. Inside was a tiny hammer attached to a string that ran up the medium's leg. Cleverly using a free hand, the medium pulled on the string to create a knock.

In the cartoon, the female medium eases the toe of her shoe under a leg of the table and, together with pressure from her hand, controls the table's movement.

Special séance tables were sold that had a spring-controlled wood block hidden on the underside of the tabletop. The medium created the raps by pushing up on the mechanism with her knee.

## GLOWING SPIRIT TRUMPETS

When séances were conducted in complete darkness, glow-in-the-dark paint containing phosphorus came in handy. This chemical absorbs and stores light. After it's returned to the dark, it releases the stored light as a glow. Fake mediums coated objects with the paint. These included musical instruments, fake hands, and cut-out stars.

To create the flying trumpet effect, the medium or an assistant held the painted horn. As the person moved around the dark room dressed in black, sitters believed that invisible spirits were making the object float. The effect was reinforced when the instrument played.

Investigators exposed the trick by secretly rubbing a black material on the trumpet's mouthpiece when it was lying on the table at the beginning of the séance. After the lights came back on, the telltale black mouth of the medium or assistant revealed the fraud.

Mediums who were adept at ventriloquism convinced sitters that a spirit was speaking through the trumpet. In another trick, an assistant spoke through a small hole in the ceiling above the séance table.

Lightweight aluminum trumpets later became available in stores that catered to magicians and mediums. These had joints that let the medium bend it for easy concealment under clothing.

To make objects appear to float, this medium uses a stick to hold a tambourine above the table. He is tied to his chair to prove to sitters that he hasn't moved. This photograph was staged in the early 1900s to reveal one way the trick was done. The room would be dark in an actual séance. Mediums also attached cardboard shapes and faces coated in glowing paint to sticks and collapsible poles that could extend up to 8 feet (2.4 m).

# CHAPTER THREE
# ABRACADABRA

*"Medium and conjuror means the same thing."*
*—John Nevil Maskelyne, 1875*

Another set of siblings was about to take the spiritualism world by storm.

Ira and William Davenport were just a few years younger than the Foxes. They lived in Buffalo, New York, about 75 miles (121 km) west of Rochester, where Maggie and Katie Fox had begun their public career.

By 1850, when the boys were eleven and nine, the sisters' spirit knockings had become famous throughout the state. Around that time, the Davenports' policeman father invited neighbors into the house to witness the boys' special powers.

The brothers' hands and feet were tied securely with rope. Then the room was darkened. After the lights came back on, visitors were amazed to see that objects had moved to different places in the room. The boys had, too. Yet they were both still tied up.

How did this happen? Mr. Davenport said that the spirits had done it. And people believed him.

Paying customers came to the house to see for themselves.

The family took advantage of the growing curiosity about spirit communication to bring in more people. In 1855, the

Ira (1839–1911) (left) and William Davenport (1841–1877) in a photograph taken around 1870. Late in life, Ira claimed that his parents always believed the brothers had "super-human power." This is doubtful. It was Mr. Davenport who taught his young sons how to escape from tied ropes. After years of practice, Ira and William improved on the rope tricks they'd learned as children.

Davenports rented a large hall, and the teenage brothers began giving public performances. After Ira and William called up the spirits, the ghosts created rapping sounds, made tables tilt, and played musical instruments.

Their séance program became so popular that the two brothers headed off on a traveling tour through the US and Canada. Ira and William were young and handsome, their show astonished audiences, and soon they were filling auditoriums.

## THE SPIRIT CABINET

The brothers added a new feature to their séance—the Spirit Cabinet. The cabinet was a large wooden box with three doors across the front. Cut in the top of the middle door was a diamond-shape opening covered inside by a small curtain.

To convince the crowd that no trickery was involved, two audience volunteers were invited to examine the Spirit Cabinet. Then they tied the brothers' wrists with rope, usually with their arms behind the back. Ira and William sat far apart on benches

A nineteenth-century print shows the inside of the Davenport brothers' Spirit Cabinet. An audience volunteer sits between the brothers to verify that they don't move from their benches. A tambourine has landed on his head. The Davenports performed their Spirit Cabinet show until William's sudden death in July 1877 while they were touring in Australia.

inside the cabinet. To secure them to the bench, the rope was pushed through holes in the seats down to the brothers' ankles, which were also bound. Sometimes an audience member sat between Ira and William to verify that they didn't move and that no one else entered the cabinet.

The Davenports' assistants placed a collection of musical instruments (guitar, violin, handbells, tambourine, trumpet) inside the cabinet and closed the doors. The gas lights in the room or auditorium were lowered.

Moments later, the audience heard each of the musical instruments playing. Hands reached through the hole at the top of the middle door. The bells and trumpet flew out of the opening. Inside the cabinet, the volunteer sitting between the brothers felt the tambourine land on his head. Fingers touched his face.

When an assistant swung open the cabinet doors, Ira and William were still tied to their benches with their hands and feet bound. The bewildered volunteer next to them insisted that the brothers never moved inside the dark cabinet. Because the cabinet sat above the floor on supports, the audience saw that no one could enter except through the front doors.

People were astounded. What had created the racket inside the Spirit Cabinet?

Ira (far left) and William (far right) Davenport pose with partner William Fay (second from left) and assistant Robert Cooper in a photograph likely taken in the late 1860s while the Davenport brothers were performing in Europe.

Buffalo-native Fay (1839–1921) managed the brothers' appearances starting in the late 1850s. He participated in performances and stood in for William, who frequently suffered from poor health.

Cooper (ca. 1820–?), a British spiritualist, wrote a book in 1867 about his seven months with the Davenport brothers while they toured Europe. In it, Cooper stated that he had seen no sign "to indicate that they [the Davenports] were anything but passive instruments, the manifestations being produced by a power outside themselves."

The Davenports fooled Cooper into believing the spirits had performed the tricks. But other Davenport assistants weren't so easily deceived.

The Davenports led audiences to believe that spirits played the instruments and tossed them outside. Not only did the spirits touch the volunteer's face, but they also stuck their ghostly hands and arms through the hole in the cabinet door.

Spiritualists lauded the Davenports as gifted mediums who could call the spirits into the cabinet whenever they wished. The flying instruments and materialized hands were proof of the spirit world.

In August 1864, the Davenport brothers took their Spirit Cabinet to Europe. The American Civil War (1861–1865) and its upheaval had made travel and performing more complicated for them at home.

During their four years touring European countries, Ira and William gave public séances as well as private ones in the homes of the wealthy. Their spirit shows became so celebrated that the brothers were invited to perform for Great Britain's Queen Victoria, Russia's Czar Alexander II, and France's Emperor Napoleon III.

Ira and William let their act speak for itself. They never directly claimed to be mediums. Yet their appearances brought

# ST. GEORGE'S HALL,

### LANGHAM PLACE.

## RETURN
##### OF THE
# BROTHERS DAVENPORT
##### AND
# MR. FAY.

THE BROTHERS DAVENPORT and Mr. FAY have the honour to announce that, after a tour of three years over the greater part of the Continent of Europe, they have returned once more, and probably for the last time, to this Metropolis, where they will give a few *Séances* previous to their departure for the United States.

During their European tour they have given *Séances* in Paris, Berlin, Vienna, Moscow, St. Petersburgh, and nearly every great Continental Capital; and have had the honour of appearing before their Majesties the Emperors of France and Russia, the Royal Family of Prussia, and great numbers of the most Distinguished Personages in Europe. Many thousands of persons of the highest rank and intelligence have witnessed the astonishing experiments given in their presence.

Throughout the Northern American States, from 1853 until their first visit to England in 1864, they were seen by hundreds of thousands of persons.

In England, their first *Séance* was given in private, to a most distinguished party of men of science and letters, who gave their most unequivocal testimony to the excellence and perfection of their experiments.

Two *Séances* of the BROTHERS DAVENPORT and Mr. FAY will be given at

## ST. GEORGE'S HALL, LANGHAM PLACE,

### On THURSDAY EVENING, APRIL 23rd,

### And SATURDAY EVENING, APRIL 25th, 1868,

#### at Eight o'clock.

**STALLS, - 3s.**          **BALCONY, - 2s.**

## ADMISSION,     ONE SHILLING.

This advertisement promoted an April 1868 appearance by the Brothers Davenport and Mr. Fay at a London theater. After four years, their *Séances* program had become famous in Europe. The text tells readers that "hundreds of thousands of persons" had seen them perform in North America between 1853 and 1864. Their show was popular among both spiritualists and skeptics.

publicity and new attention to spiritualism, persuading many people that spirits truly existed.

Magicians smelled a trick.

## A SECRET REVEALED

In spring 1865, an amateur magician in Cheltenham, England, went to see the brothers perform. During a morning show in his hometown, twenty-five-year-old John Nevil Maskelyne volunteered to be one of the audience members who came onstage to confirm that the brothers were effectively tied up.

The townhall's windows were covered with curtains to keep the stage shadowy and spooky. But at a crucial moment in the brothers' performance, one curtain briefly fell away. The keen-eyed Maskelyne was standing next to the cabinet. The sudden light on the darkened stage allowed him to glimpse Ira Davenport inside holding a musical instrument. Ira's hand was free of the ropes.

Realizing that the Davenports were skilled escape artists rather than gifted mediums, Maskelyne announced to the audience that he had seen how the brothers pulled off their cabinet séance. He declared that he would perform the same tricks for the Cheltenham crowd in the near future.

The Davenports didn't appreciate Maskelyne's pronouncement, but at least he hadn't given away their secret.

Within three months, Maskelyne and his friend George Cooke, a carpenter and fellow amateur magician, developed an extraordinary illusion based on the Davenport Spirit Cabinet. Maskelyne climbed into a wooden box. With help from audience volunteers, the box was locked and tied with rope. Next it was lifted into the cabinet, and the doors were shut.

When the cabinet doors were reopened after a few minutes, the audience was stunned to see Maskelyne sitting on top of the locked and bound box.

Maskelyne and Cooke went on to develop even more remarkable illusions based on the Spirit Cabinet. They attracted both magic lovers and devoted spiritualists to their shows. Some spiritualists claimed that the two performers were mediums, just like the Davenports. Maskelyne knew the truth. It was all magic and hocus-pocus.

# ECYPTIAN HALL.
## MASKELYNE AND COOKE

ENGLAND'S HOME OF MYSTERY.

EVERY EVENING AT EIGHT O' CLOCK & SATURDAYS AT 3 & 8.

SCREVINS IN TWO PIECES. THE SENSATION OF LONDON. W. MORTON MANAGER.

# MODERN SPIRITUALISM
## BY J.N. MASKELYNE.

A MOONLIGHT TRANSIT OF VENUS

LONDON: FREDERICK WARNE & C?.

# MODERN SPIRITUALISM.

A SHORT ACCOUNT OF ITS RISE
AND PROGRESS, WITH SOME EXPOSURES
OF SO-CALLED SPIRIT MEDIA.

BY

## JOHN NEVIL MASKELYNE,
ILLUSIONIST AND ANTI-SPIRITUALIST.

LONDON:
FOR THE AUTHOR BY
FREDERICK WARNE AND CO.,
BEDFORD STREET, STRAND.
New York: SCRIBNER, WELFORD, AND ARMSTRONG.

He later wrote that, at the moment onstage with the Davenports in 1865, "I got a key to the *knotty* problem, which I ever since used . . . to reproduce all the tricks of the Brothers."

Maskelyne eventually became one of the world's most renowned magicians and inventors of illusions. Throughout his career, he kept up a campaign to expose fake mediums whom he considered to be no more than conjurers pretending to have special powers. He believed they were misleading the public and making money doing it. Besides that, their séances cut into the stage business of honest magicians.

In Maskelyne's opinion, these fraudsters weren't particularly good at it, either. He once said that a mediocre magician could perform the same tricks as a medium and get away with the deceit. "There does not exist, and there never has existed," wrote Maskelyne in 1891, "a professed 'medium' of any note who has not been convicted of trickery or fraud."

## LOST LOVED ONES

By the time the Davenport brothers sailed for home in September 1868, they had spread the ideas of spiritualism to thousands in Europe. John Nevil Maskelyne acknowledged that "the Brothers did more than all other men to familiarize England with the so-called *Spiritualism*."

Back in the United States, interest in spiritualism had grown since the Davenports departed four years earlier, thanks to the tragedy of war.

Even President Abraham Lincoln had hosted a widely publicized White House séance during the Civil War. His wife, Mary Todd Lincoln, believed in spiritualism. She had previously attended a séance in hopes of communicating with her son Willie, who had died of typhoid fever in February 1862.

In April 1863, Mrs. Lincoln arranged for a medium to come to the White House Red Room one evening. The president, though not a spiritualist himself, went along with the séance. The sitters included the Lincolns, the secretaries of war and the navy, three friends, and a reporter invited by the president.

The medium called for the spirits, and they made themselves known in the dimly lit room. The ghosts pinched one man's ears and pulled on another's beard. Tables in the room and a painting on the wall moved.

After an hour, the group heard loud knocking under President Lincoln's feet. The medium, who seemed to be in a trance, announced that the spirits wanted to communicate. He asked for blank paper and a pencil to be laid on the séance table. Then he covered them with a guest's handkerchief.

There was more rapping. The medium quickly pulled off the handkerchief, revealing a message on the paper: "Make a bold front and fight the enemy." It was signed by Henry Knox, an American Revolution general and the nation's first secretary of war. Knox had died nearly sixty years before.

The president asked the spirits about the raging war. "Tell us when this rebellion will be put down."

The medium placed a fresh paper under the handkerchief as before, and the group waited. When the medium pulled off the handkerchief, Knox's written response was there. He had consulted with spirits of other celebrated generals, including George Washington and Marquis de Lafayette of the American Revolution, as well as the Frenchman Napoleon Bonaparte. The spirits gave their opinions: "Concentrate your forces upon one point . . . The rebellion will die of exhaustion . . . The end [is] approaching."

# SPIRITUALISM AT THE WHITE HOUSE.

---

# Napoleon, Lafayette, Washington, Franklin, Douglas, and Henry Knox on the Conduct of the War.

---

## Some Good Advice from the Other World.

---

Correspondence of the Boston G: **sett** .
WASHINGTON, **April** 23, 1863.

In April 1863, at the height of the Civil War, a *Boston Gazette* writer reported on a séance at the White House. The story was carried in dozens of newspapers across the country. This headline is from the *Weekly Pioneer and Democrat* of Saint Paul, MN, on June 12, 1863.

Lincoln commented, with some skepticism, "Their talk and advices sound very much like the talk of my Cabinet."

When the war finally ended in 1865, perhaps as many as 750,000 soldiers had died from wounds and disease, according to estimates. President Lincoln himself was shot and killed by an assassin in April 1865. Many soldiers remained missing in action. Every town was touched, and mourners were desperate to communicate with their dead loved ones or to learn the fate of those lost. Spiritualism attracted a multitude of new followers.

With so much death, many people found solace in the idea that these souls lived on in the spirit world and could be contacted. During séances, some mediums fell into a trance and spoke in the voice of a dead soldier, explaining when and where he was killed. In other cases, ghosts communicated in writing by using the medium's hand.

Some spiritualists claimed that by 1870, there were 11 million believers in America. At more than a quarter of the country's population, that number was probably exaggerated. Still, séances and mediums had definitely gained in popularity since the war broke out in 1861.

In 1870, spiritualist Emma Hardinge wrote about the Civil War's aftermath: "Never in any period of its [spiritualism's] brief history has it taken so deep and fervent a hold upon the hearts of a mourning people."

## IT'S MAGIC!

When the Davenports set out on their next United States tour, they were able to travel by train to more towns and cities across the country than ever before. The Transcontinental Railroad was completed in 1869, and new rail lines were constantly being built.

In 1869 at a stop in La Crosse, Wisconsin, they hired twenty-year-old Harry Kellar to organize their tours and handle expenses and box office cash. Kellar discovered that Ira and William, not the spirits, created the mysterious activity inside the Spirit Cabinet. He learned how they managed to escape knotted ropes in seconds, and he secretly practiced the trick.

Kellar's ambition was to be a successful magician. After four

Harry Kellar (1849–1922) in a portrait from around 1892. Kellar enjoyed a long career into the twentieth century and became a much beloved and admired conjurer. He performed on six continents and was the first American-born magician to gain worldwide celebrity.

years as an assistant with the brothers, he left them in 1873 to start his own traveling magic show. The Davenports' partner, William Fay, went with him. Forming their own act, "Fay and Kellar," they made the Spirit Cabinet a key part of their show.

The pair toured together for two years until the summer of 1875. While sailing to Europe on an ocean steamer, their ship hit rocks off the coast of France. Kellar and Fay lost their props and costumes in the shipwreck. Down on their luck and low on cash, they went their separate ways. Fay returned to the Davenports. Kellar replaced his equipment and resumed his act.

The young magician continued to incorporate séance tricks into his show. Kellar didn't pretend to be a medium. He told audiences that the sounds and objects coming from within the cabinet were part of a magic trick. No ghosts were involved.

In fact, he announced that he could perform *all* the wonders that occurred during a séance. Kellar challenged anyone to tie him up inside the Spirit Cabinet. Spiritualists and the curious paid to see if he could escape the knots.

One time a spiritualist used 11 feet (3.4 m) of rope to tie Kellar's hands together with special sailor's knots. The Spirit Cabinet doors were shut. Usually, he escaped in seconds. Nearly a minute clicked by. The audience became restless. Had Kellar been defeated?

Finally he pushed open the doors and held up his hands, completely free of the rope. The escape had been so difficult that the rope cut the skin on his wrists. Once again, Kellar proved that magic, not ghosts, was the secret behind the Spirit Cabinet.

Kellar's cabinet séances were more elaborate and entertaining than those of the Davenport brothers. His performances brought in crowds wherever he traveled throughout the US, Mexico, South America, Australia, and Europe.

Maskelyne, Kellar, and other magicians demonstrated to audiences that they could create the same phenomena on stage that spiritualists were producing during séances. People became suspicious of séances, and they lost trust in mediums.

Yet magician tricks failed to sway devout spiritualists. Their beliefs stayed as strong as ever. Soon startling events would test their faith.

Using what he learned from Ira and William Davenport, Harry Kellar included the Spirit Cabinet in his magic show. The 1894 advertising poster for Kellar's Perplexing Cabinet highlighted ghosts, skeletons, and devilish imps to make the cabinet seem more mysterious. His show included the same phenomena seen at séances: table tipping, knocking, materializations, spirit writing, and mind reading.

Kellar never pretended to have supernatural powers or contact with the spirit world. Like all good magicians, he controlled what his audience saw. He used sleight of hand and special illusions while he directed his viewers' attention elsewhere.

# HOW DID THEY DO IT?

## BROTHERS OR GHOSTS?

Ira and William Davenport were experts at pretending to be mediums. They were also adept at escaping knotted ropes. No matter how well the audience volunteers bound them, the brothers worked their hands free. If one brother was tied too tightly, the other was able to slip out of the knots and help. "There was one chance in twenty million to hold us both at the same time," Ira said years after the brothers stopped performing.

With their freed hands, the brothers strummed the guitar, shook the tambourine, jingled the handbells, and tooted the trumpet. One of them touched the volunteer's face and laid the tambourine atop his head. Finished with their mischief, Ira and William slipped their hands back into the knots before their assistant opened the cabinet doors.

As an elderly man, Ira admitted that the key to the Davenports' successful act was their knot-escape trick, their physical dexterity, and some slippery Vaseline rubbed onto their hands and wrists.

# WILLIAM MUMLER AND THE SPIRIT PHOTOGRAPHS

William Mumler (1832–1884) was born in Boston and worked as a metal engraver there, specializing in jewelry. Photography was his hobby. In the fall of 1862, after creating a self-portrait, he claimed to notice a young girl's body in the photograph sitting next to him. Mumler said she was his cousin who had died a dozen years before.

He showed the image to a spiritualist friend, and the man declared it to be proof that spirits exist and are visible to the human eye. The spiritualist community proclaimed Mumler a medium whose gifts enabled him to reveal ghostly figures hovering close to the people he photographed. Mumler denied knowing how the spirits appeared in his photographs.

People hired Mumler to produce images of the ghosts of their cherished husbands, children, and wives. As spirit photography became more popular, other photographers offered the special portraits, too.

When a man spotted his very-much-alive wife as a ghost in one of Mumler's spirit photographs, Mumler was accused of fraud. His ghosts often turned out to be images of well-known people (living and dead) or those who had previously come to his studio for regular portraits. The word got out to the Boston spiritualists, and they backed away from him.

After these revelations damaged his reputation in his hometown, Mumler took his business to New York City where he sold hundreds of his spirit photographs for $10 each (about $200 today). But the New York police received complaints from customers, and by the end of 1868, Mumler was arrested for fraud.

At his spring 1869 trial, several professional photographers explained ways that Mumler might have created his spirit photographs by using tricks during the development process. In the 1860s, photography was relatively new. Most people were unaware of the ways that a photograph could

William Mumler created this spirit photograph for Mrs. Tinkham in his Boston studio. It appears to show the ghost of the woman's young daughter resting her arm on her mother.

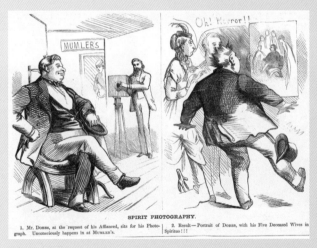

This cartoon appeared in *Harper's Weekly* magazine in May 1869, poking fun at William Mumler and his spirit photography. A man sits for his portrait at Mumler's studio. When he later returns with his fiancée to view the printed photograph, they are both horrified to see ghosts of the man's five dead wives hovering around him in the picture.

be manipulated to show objects or people that weren't actually there.

Mumler had support from spiritualists and other photographers who claimed the ghosts were genuine. At the end of his trial, the judge released him, saying that the prosecution had failed to prove that Mumler intentionally deceived his customers.

Back in Boston again, Mumler reopened his business. He also advertised spirit photographs through the mail. If a customer sent information about a loved one to him with $7.50 (about $150 today), he returned a spirit photo in three weeks.

Believers in spiritualism ignored the accusations of fraud. They treasured the photographs Mumler provided. In their view, spirit photography was a new technology that revealed what mortals couldn't see, and it provided solid proof that the dead remain with us.

William Mumler continued to work with photography techniques. In the late 1870s, he discovered a method that made it easier to reproduce photographs on newsprint. His "Mumler Process" contributed to the revolutionary change in the appearance of newspapers, which had been restricted to using illustrations.

This spirit photograph appeared in the front of an 1891 book that John Nevil Maskelyne cowrote. It shows the ghost of Maskelyne, who was far from dead, standing before his coauthor, Dr. Lionel Weatherly. In the book, the authors argue against the existence of spirits and other supernatural phenomena.

In 1872, Mary Todd Lincoln visited Mumler's Boston studio, and he made this spirit photograph for her. It shows the ghost of her husband, President Abraham Lincoln, standing behind her with his hands on her shoulders. Lincoln had been assassinated in April 1865.

In 1863, French photographer Eugène Thiébault (1826–1880) used double exposure techniques to create a spirit image of magician Henri Robin (1811–1874) embraced by a ghost. Robin used the Davenport brothers' spiritualism tricks in his Paris show.

# CHAPTER FOUR
## SUSPICIOUS SÉANCES

"What fools are they who still pretend to believe against all this evidence!"
—*Maggie Fox Kane, 1888*

On a March evening in 1884, George Morse took his seat in the front row at a Philadelphia séance. The young man had already attended five séances with the medium Henry Gordon.

The room on the building's second floor contained an organ, a spirit cabinet, and a couple dozen seats set up in rows. A gaslight hung from the ceiling and an oil lamp burned in the corner. Both were turned down low, making the room almost completely dark. Morse could barely make out the face of the person sitting next to him.

Visitors had paid $1 (about $30 today) to attend the séance. Many were desperate to see and perhaps be tenderly touched by a lost loved one. On this particular evening, Thomas Hazard was there. Thirty years before, he had become involved with spiritualism after his wife died. Since then, his five daughters had gone to the grave, too. Only his son survived.

After everyone was seated, the séance began. Henry Gordon stepped into the spirit cabinet. His assistant played a hymn on the organ and encouraged the small audience to sing. As the song ended, the cabinet door opened.

A white figure seemed to float from the cabinet. Hazard gasped. He thought it was his daughter Esther, who had died just four years before at age thirty-two.

George Morse jumped from his front row seat and grabbed the ghost. Shocked, Hazard reached for his daughter's spirit to protect her. But Morse had already tackled the ghost to the floor. He pulled off the spirit's wig and mask.

It was Henry Gordon dressed in a white nightgown and lace.

Morse wasn't an ordinary séance sitter. He was a newspaper journalist investigating Henry Gordon, who he suspected was deceiving his customers.

Morse brought along a fellow reporter and an undercover detective to the séance, both posing as his friends. They helped subdue Gordon and his organ-playing assistant, who were arrested for fraud. The evidence against them included fake beards, wigs, dresses, and other clothing found in the medium's spirit cabinet. Gordon had used the costumes to disguise himself as the ghosts of his clients' departed friends and family.

One of the women attending the séance realized for the first time that she'd been deceived by Gordon. "I see now that the whole thing was a fraud," she told Morse, "although when I stepped up to [the spirit] cabinet and saw the faces it seemed to me that I recognized them as those of relatives."

From his previous visits to the medium's séance room, Morse learned firsthand how Gordon obtained information about his clients. At one visit, the reporter told Gordon a made-up story

Fake mediums who specialized in materialization séances offered a spirit's bodily appearance. But like the ghost in this 1922 staged photograph, the spirit was the result of the medium's tricks: costumes, wigs, masks, black clothing, and luminous paint.

about a woman named Ellen whom he adored. She had tragically died right before they were to be married, he said.

During the next séance Morse attended, Ellen's ghost appeared in the dim light. She told Morse that she still loved him. As she leaned close and gently touched him, the reporter smelled mutton stew on her body. He knew it was the disguised medium, not the spirit of an imaginary dead fiancée.

Henry Gordon had used the same technique on Thomas Hazard. By drawing out personal details during séance visits, Gordon discovered that Hazard had a deceased daughter named Esther.

## NEW MANIFESTATIONS

After journalists, magicians, and other skeptics exposed the methods for producing table tipping and rapping, the public had become suspicious of those spiritualism phenomena. Fake mediums were forced to find more mysterious ways to keep people believing in their séances.

Like Henry Gordon, many of them adopted the spirit cabinet, made famous by the Davenports and several magicians. Mediums also developed new techniques to demonstrate the presence of a spirit.

### MATERIALIZATION

Mediums claimed that a spirit could collect enough material from the sitters or the medium to become visible. Such a materialization, spiritualists said, was tangible proof of the spirit world.

Materialization séances became popular, with some mediums specializing in them. Sitters were invited into a nearly dark room. The medium entered a cabinet, closed the door, and soon the spirits appeared.

The ghosts seemed to gaze lovingly at sitters and even touched them. Sitters were certain they had seen the spirit of a dead relative.

### SPIRIT WRITING

In the 1880s, spirit guides became common at séances. The guide took over when the medium went into a trance.

The trance began as the medium's eyes slowly closed. Her breathing changed, becoming faster. Her head moved back and forth, her hands opened and closed, her face twitched, she trembled. Then she sat still, seemingly entranced.

Mediums claimed that when they were under a trance and a spirit guide was in control, they became a channel through which the spirits sent messages. If the message was verbal, the medium's voice changed, often developing an accent that matched the guide's nationality. Sometimes the message appeared by automatic writing as the entranced medium's hand moved a pen across paper.

Another communication method was the planchette. The medium, alone or with sitters, lightly placed their fingers on the heart-shaped wooden device. If they concentrated, energy from the spirit world flowed through their fingers and moved the planchette. The pencil attached to it wrote the spirit's message on a sheet of paper.

In 1890, the Ouija talking board was introduced to the American public to do the same thing without the pencil and paper. The boards were sold to mediums, people who held private séances at home, and to those who used them as a game or toy.

Mediums added planchettes to their séances to spell out the spirits' messages. Users lightly rested their fingertips on top of the wooden planchette. A question was asked. As the planchette's wheels moved across a sheet of paper, the pencil wrote the answer. This was a nineteenth-century advertisement.

Ouija boards are based on the original planchettes but eliminate the need for paper and pencil. Instead, the message appears as the hole in the device stops over each letter or word (yes, no).

## SLATE WRITING

Beginning in the 1860s, American medium Henry Slade became known for receiving spirit messages through slate writing. A tall, handsome man, Slade used small rectangular slates common in schools at the time.

After showing that a slate was clean, he encouraged the sitters to ask the spirits a question. Slade held the slate beneath the edge of the table along with a piece of slate pencil, similar to chalk. He told sitters that the spirits were more likely to work in darkness, which is why he dimmed the lights and held the slate under the table.

Within moments, sitters heard scratching on the slate. Slade announced that it was a spirit writing an answer. After he dramatically revealed the slate, the sitters saw a handwritten message.

In another version of slate writing, he tied two blank slates together face-to-face with a piece of slate pencil or chalk between them. After he placed the slates atop the table, a sitter asked a question. Soon the group heard a scratching sound. When Slade separated the slates, a written message was visible on one of them.

Curious people paid for spirit writing séances, many hoping for important messages from dead loved ones. But Slade's slate writing had nothing to do with spirits.

In 1876, he was exposed in London when some sitters snatched a slate from him in the dark and found a message written before they'd even asked a question. Slade was brought to trial for cheating the public. John Nevil Maskelyne testified as a witness against him, and the magician demonstrated spirit-writing tricks in court. Slade lost his case, but he fled England before he could be jailed.

Despite his exposure, Slade continued his career elsewhere in the world. Slate writing developed into a popular form of spirit communication adopted by many mediums.

## THE SEYBERT COMMISSION

By 1884 when journalist George Morse exposed the medium Henry Gordon in Philadelphia, spiritualism had become increasingly controversial. Believers were convinced that

Henry Slade (1835–1905) was a medium who specialized in slate writing. Despite being caught several times tricking his audience and being famously arrested in 1876, Slade continued his work as a medium throughout the world. He managed to fool other investigators but not the Seybert Commission. Slade became an alcoholic, and his health failed. He died in a Michigan sanitorium. Some say that he eventually confessed to faking his séances and slate writing.

A 1920 illustration shows a man in a trance supposedly receiving spirit messages.

mediums called spirits to séances. The phenomena of knocking, table tipping, materializations, automatic writing, and slate writing confirmed the spirits' presence.

Skeptics needed better proof before they would accept spiritualism. They charged that mediums used the same tools as a magician to fool their audience: making up a story that distracts or persuades, misdirecting attention away from the deception, and acting a part. In fact, the skeptics pointed out, some mediums had earlier careers as stage performers. For the doubters to be convinced, a medium had to prove that he or she was *not* using tricks.

Spiritualists conceded that a magician was capable of imitating the actions of the spirits. And they also admitted that a few dishonest, greedy mediums had practiced deception. But that did not mean that *all* mediums were fakes. "The most severe blows that Spiritualism has sustained," wrote one spiritualist, "have been those aimed by unprincipled and avaricious mediums."

Many from both sides wanted to settle the debate with a scientific analysis of spiritualism and mediums. Spiritualist Henry Seybert decided to fund a formal study conducted by a group of reputable academics. Shortly before his death in 1883, he gave money to the University of Pennsylvania in Philadelphia to appoint the Seybert Commission for Investigating Modern Spiritualism.

The commission of ten men included physicians, scientists, and professors—most associated with the university. Seybert's personal friend and fellow spiritualist was named as an advisor to recommend mediums for testing. He was Thomas Hazard, father of Esther, the ghost daughter at Henry Gordon's séance.

The commission members vowed that they were neutral in their opinion of spiritualism and would do their best to investigate thoroughly by collecting evidence and basing their conclusions "solely on our own observations."

## SLATES, RAPS, AND GHOSTS

Starting its work in 1884, the commission controlled conditions at the examined séances as much as the mediums would allow. Several members attended each séance so that multiple viewpoints and impressions were included in the observations.

In their report, which was published three years later, the commission members stated that some mediums invited to participate either refused to meet with the commission or demanded money. The commission considered that a bribe.

Several mediums who agreed to be tested weren't able to produce *any* supernatural phenomena. They claimed that the spirits wouldn't cooperate in the negative atmosphere created by doubters on the commission.

Henry Slade was one medium who submitted to testing. But after the commission met with him, the members decided that his slate writing was "fraudulent throughout. There was really no need of any elaborate method of investigation; close observation was all that was required."

They found that Slade had written messages on slates before the séance started. During the séance, he used sleight of hand to switch slates. One of the investigators held a small mirror under the table to spot the switch.

To study rappings, the commission invited Maggie Fox Kane to be part of the study. During two séances with her, she informed the group that the spirit of Henry Seybert was communicating with them.

One of the members asked, "Is he satisfied with the Commission?"

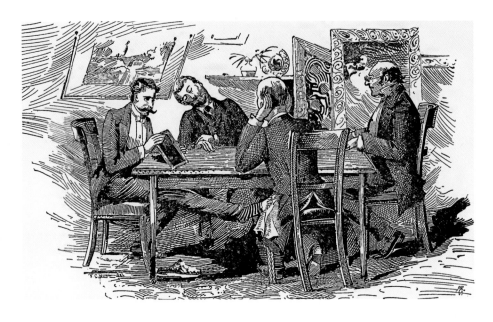

This cartoon appeared in an 1891 book cowritten by magician John Nevil Maskelyne. It depicts three German scientists investigating slate-writing medium Henry Slade in 1878. Maskelyne believed this group had been duped by Slade partly because they were unfamiliar with the magic tricks he used.

Someone wrote down the alphabet and pointed to each letter as the message emerged. Seybert's knocks spelled out: "I will be satisfied before the investigation is through."

When Maggie's feet were touching the wooden floor, commission members heard rapping noises in response to questions. To test whether the sound was audible when her feet did not contact wood, they asked Maggie to stand on glass tumblers as the spirits replied to questions.

Although she insisted she heard the knocks, no one else did.

The investigators determined that Maggie's "so-called raps are confined wholly to her person," likely her feet. When the sound of her cracking joints couldn't reverberate through the wood floor, the spirits were silent.

The commission offered to attend another séance with her, which might change their conclusion that the raps came from her, not spirits. Maggie declined, saying that her health interfered with her work and that the manifestations had been "unsatisfactory."

The materializations of ghosts didn't impress the commission, either. During one séance, the attending members heard voices. The medium announced that several spirits were in the room. The commission report noted that the whispers never occurred at the same time the medium was speaking and they all sounded as if they were made by the same voice—the medium's.

At a different séance in which a spirit cabinet was used, a faceless human form emerged from the cabinet draped in a cloth that shined in the dark room. When a committee member touched the drapery, he felt soft silk netting. The ghost brushed against his face, and the man smelled phosphorus, the chemical in glow-in-the-dark paint.

One investigator wrote in the commission's report that he had seen no proof that a spirit could be materialized. "In only two instances have any Spirits professed to be members of my family, and in one of those two instances, as it happened, that member was alive and in robust health, and in the other a Spirit claimed a fictitious relationship, that of niece."

## UNPERSUADED

The Seybert Commission investigation, funded by a spiritualist, had determined that every tested medium had used obvious deceptions. The secretary of the commission wrote, "I have been forced to the conclusion that Spiritualism . . . presents the melancholy spectacle of gross fraud, perpetrated upon an uncritical portion of the community."

In the report, the chairman of the commission, H. H. Furness, explained how fraudulent mediums were able to fool their sitters. People are overcome by the environment of the séance and fail to notice obvious fakery, he wrote. Furness listed "the darkened room; the music; the singing" as factors. Sitters are also influenced by being surrounded by others who believe that what is happening is supernatural.

Spiritualists strongly objected to the commission's report. They alleged that the group only examined mediums who had previously been exposed as frauds. Besides, some commission members, despite what they claimed, already had a bias against spiritualism before beginning the investigation. One spiritualist lamented, "There is no doubt that the report of the Seybert Commission set back for the time the cause of psychic truth."

Magicians noted that neither the commission members nor other spiritualism investigators were trained to spot all the tricks used by mediums. It took a skillful conjurer to expose the more talented fake mediums. As evidence of this, magicians pointed to the commission's observation of Harry Kellar.

At the time of the investigation, Kellar was performing his stage show in Philadelphia. Several commission members asked him to privately demonstrate his slate-writing trick. To control the test, they brought nine clean slates for him to use.

Instead of duplicating Slade's tricks, Kellar performed one of his own. The messages that mysteriously appeared on the commission's slates were written in seven languages. Despite carefully watching his actions, the members couldn't figure out how he'd pulled it off. In their report, they stated that Kellar's slate-writing was "far more remarkable than any which we have witnessed with Mediums."

Magician John Nevil Maskelyne wasn't surprised. After reading the Seybert Commission report, he commented that spiritualism had "received its most deadly wound through the

This advertising poster from 1895 shows Harry Kellar's Fly-To illusion, which was based on the Davenport Spirit Cabinet. A woman was locked inside a cage, and its curtains were drawn. When Kellar opened the curtains again, she had vanished. She reappeared in a matching cage hanging 10 feet (3 m) above the stage.

means which, it was fondly hoped, would place it once and for ever upon a sure and solid foundation that would withstand every shock which unbelief could bring against it."

An even greater shock was on the horizon.

## THE DEATH BLOW

In spring 1888, Maggie Fox Kane, then in her midfifties, announced, "Spiritualism is a curse." The following October, she went even further. Before an audience of 2,000 people in New York City, she confessed that she had misled everyone about her powers as a medium. Her sister Kate was there in support of the admission.

Maggie read a statement, which was published in the *New York World* and newspapers throughout the country. Recognizing her role in perpetuating spiritualism, she said, "After my sister Katie and I expose it, I hope Spiritualism will be given a death blow." She went on to declare, "I never believed in the spirits, and I never professed to be a Spiritualist."

Taking off her right shoe, she demonstrated exactly how she could produce a rapping sound loud enough to be heard throughout the theater. She explained that she used her lower leg muscles to control movement of the toe and ankle bones. Doctors in the audience came up to the stage and felt her foot as she produced the knocking. They confirmed what she said.

Maggie admitted that she and Kate started the rapping "just for the fun of the thing." At first the sisters created the haunting sounds by sending an apple bumping up and down on the wooden floor. Then they discovered they could produce the knocking by cracking their knuckle and toe joints. Their mother was the one who believed "it was the spirits that were speaking," Maggie said. "We were too young and too simple to imagine such a thing."

But their prank soon got out of hand. "So many persons had heard the 'rappings,'" she explained, "that we could not confess the wrong without exciting very great anger on the part of those we had deceived. So we went right on."

According to Maggie, her sister Leah knew that the spirit rapping was a hoax. In fact, the girls showed her how they rapped with their feet.

Leah saw a way to make money from the public interest in

her younger sisters, and she took control of the two girls' lives. She forced their parents into telling a story about the rapping beginnings that Leah and her spiritualist friends later used to promote their new religion.

Maggie claimed that at séances, Leah directed the girls with a signal when to rap "yes," when to rap "no." She and Katie weren't old enough to deceive so many people without Leah's help. "I do not exaggerate in any way when I say that I have feared that woman all my life."

In criticizing those spiritualists who dishonestly preyed on others for profit, Maggie said in her statement, that spiritualism "is all a fraud, a hypocrisy, and a delusion." She was sorry for her part in the deception.

## REVELATIONS

Maggie's announcement was greeted by hisses from the spiritualists in the audience. Many others were upset to read about Maggie's confession in the newspapers, especially those who had spent thousands of dollars on mediums.

One San Francisco man wrote to her, "I am now eighty-one years old and have but a short time, of course, to remain in this world, and I feel great anxiety to know through you if I have been deceived all this time . . . Will you greatly oblige me with an answer?"

Yet even after Maggie's admission, spiritualists continued to believe that she and Kate were gifted mediums. Unfortunately, the women had troubled lives that interfered with their abilities. Some spiritualists claimed that Maggie had obviously been coerced to make the statement while she was weakened by alcoholism. Others said that she had fallen into poverty and confessed as part of a moneymaking scheme.

But whatever the reasons behind it, one spiritualist assured a reporter, "Their revelations do not affect the faith of Spiritualists."

The pressure grew on Maggie to recant, and she did a year later. Her critics said she missed her income from being a medium and couldn't afford to stick to her confession. Nevertheless, she slid into poverty.

Leah died in 1890; Maggie never forgave her. Kate died in

# DEATH OF SPIRITUALISM !

Newspapers carried accounts of Maggie Fox Kane's confession. A headline from a Georgia paper called it "Spiritualism's Downfall," and one in Nebraska announced "A Spiritualistic Expose." This headline is from the [New York] *World*, October 27, 1888.

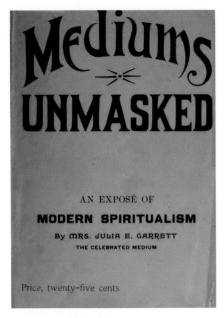

Garrett's fifty-six-page booklet contained explanations of table tipping, slate writing, and materializations. She called those who faked trances "the most heartless liars and frauds of all mediums."

This 1891 book exposed the methods used by fake mediums to fool people. Its anonymous author, A. Medium, explains in the preface that he'd worked as a medium for twenty years and wrote the book to atone for his past deceit.

1892, and Maggie in 1893, both from the effects of alcoholism.

Newspapers called Maggie's 1888 confession "a death blow to Spiritualism." More attacks on the faith were to come. In the early 1890s, several former mediums published books that explained exactly how "supernatural" phenomena were performed at a séance.

In *Mediums Unmasked*, Julia Garrett revealed the tricks of the trade, saying that she regretted her twelve years of deceit as a medium. "I know there are many good, honest people who firmly believe in Spiritualism," she wrote, "and I feel sorry when I think how mediums deceive them, for there is neither truth nor honesty in mediumship."

To warn the public of this fraud, she divulged how she had performed slate writing, materializations, trumpet talking, and fortune-telling. "No medium believes in the return of spirits, and anyone of them would, I believe, be frightened half to death at sight of a ghost."

The author of *Revelations of a Spirit Medium* remained anonymous, calling himself A. Medium. He admitted lying to people for two decades as he worked as a medium. His book was more than three hundred pages long and contained detailed explanations for the phenomena witnessed at a séance, including mind reading, fortune-telling, slate writing, rapping, and materializations of faces and bodies.

The disclosures by former mediums, newspaper exposés, and the Seybert report helped to cool the public's enthusiasm for spiritualism. Yet one editor wasn't so sure it would last. After Maggie Fox Kane's admission, he wrote, "Spiritualistic impostors will find as many fools as ever and continue to make their cheats profitable."

His prediction turned out to come true.

# HOW DID THEY DO IT?

A séance's tricks were enhanced by the medium's mesmerizing talk that suggested to sitters what they were seeing. Those inclined to believe were easily fooled. In the dark, even a skeptic had difficulty detecting exactly how a trick was done.

Seated in a séance circle with hands touching, the two sitters on either side of the medium thought they securely held her. But by clever motion, she slipped her hands away from them and connected the two sitters' hands to each other. Once free, the medium manipulated her spirit props. The sitters all assumed that she was still part of their circle.

Many mediums were exposed when someone turned on the lights and caught them out of their chair carrying items or swishing around the room dressed like a ghost.

## MATERIALIZATIONS

Mediums "materialized" the spirits by using costumes, masks, trapdoors, open windows and ladders, and assistants. Sitters were warned not to touch a materialization because of the danger to the medium. Investigators who ignored the warning discovered that a ghost was actually the flesh-and-blood medium or an assistant.

Ghostly figures often glowed in the dark. A luminous face painted on the back of a vest looked

like a spirit as the medium or assistant moved around. When the lights were on, the vest and face were easily concealed under a dark coat.

A flying ghost was a piece of filmy, thin cloth coated with glow-in-the-dark paint. The smell of the phosphorus reminded some sitters of the musty odor of a graveyard. The medium pulled the spirit up and down with a hidden pulley and thread. He used ventriloquism to convince sitters that the ghost was talking. Child spirits might be a doll or an assistant on his or her knees covered by a white robe.

## SLATE WRITING

The Seybert Commission discovered that there was always a period when the medium hid the slate from view. Often the actions occurred in a dimly lit room. After misdirecting the sitters' attention by his actions or words, the medium adeptly used sleight-of-hand to switch the slates.

The switch sometimes was performed with help from a hidden assistant. Or the medium did the switch himself with a prewritten slate that he'd placed within reach, either under his clothes, at his feet, or near his chair. Slade was caught writing a message on a slate under the table with his toes. At Slade's London trial, Maskelyne wrote on a slate with chalk held between his teeth, showing how a medium could scribble a message in the dark.

Nearly forty years after demonstrating slate writing to the Seybert Commission, conjurer Harry Kellar revealed to friends how he performed the trick. He had prepared by buying a slate of every kind sold in the city so that when the commission members arrived with their blank slates, Kellar had one that matched.

Seated around a table with Kellar, each commission member wrote a question on a slate. Kellar placed it with a tiny piece of slate pencil under the table edge. He held the slate with his thumb, his four fingers remaining visible on top of the table.

As part of the advanced preparation, his assistant was positioned in a storage area underneath the meeting room. He took the slate from under Kellar's thumb by reaching through a small trapdoor cut in the floor's carpet under the table. The assistant switched it with an identical slate on which he had written a message.

When a Seybert Commission member asked to hold a slate under the table with Kellar, it posed no problem for the magician. After a minute, in the midst of a fake cough, Kellar momentarily jerked the slate away from the man's hand. His assistant instantly replaced it with a new slate containing the message. The man, distracted by Kellar's coughing, never realized what was happening.

A demonstration of a slate writing trick staged by the magician Harry Houdini around 1923–24. A blank slate is placed on the sitter's head (Houdini's wife), an area where the medium says the spiritual energy is stronger. As the medium (Houdini) reaches up to remove the slate and show the spirit message to her, his assistant switches the blank slate with one that contains a written message. The sitter isn't aware of the assistant behind her and can't tell when the switch is made above her head.

## CHAPTER FIVE

# THE MAGICIAN AND THE SPIRITUALIST

"I saw my dead mother, as clearly as ever I saw her in life. I am a cool observer and don't make mistakes. It was wonderful."
—*Arthur Conan Doyle, 1920*

The Kansas town's opera house was standing room only. The audience had crowded inside that evening in late November 1897 to see Houdini the Great and his clairvoyant assistant, Mademoiselle Beatrice.

An athletically built young man took the stage. He announced that he had heard about the town's recent tragedy, a woman's brutal murder. The Great Houdini promised to contact the spirits to solve the heinous crime.

Everyone knew about the murder that had occurred the month before. The victim had been sitting at her sewing machine in her rural home when she was attacked. Her husband found her unconscious on the floor lying in her own blood. It was too late to save her.

The motive had apparently been theft because money had been stolen from the house. A search of the property by the sheriff and neighbors failed to find the culprit.

Mademoiselle Beatrice entered the stage dressed in lace. After the petite woman sat on a chair, Houdini blindfolded her. Then he led the crowd in a hymn as the séance began. After a few verses, Mademoiselle Beatrice slumped in the chair.

Houdini told the audience that she had fallen into a trance. As he walked back and forth across the stage, he asked her questions about the crime. How was the victim murdered?

In a slow, unemotional voice, the young woman answered, "She was stabbed seventeen times with a butcher knife."

"Was the killer an intruder?"

"No."

"So he was known to her?"

"Yes."

A murmur of nervous voices rippled through the theater. The murderer was someone the victim knew . . . someone they all probably knew!

Houdini leaned close to her. "What is the murderer's name?"

The crowd strained to hear her answer.

"His name," he said again, more forcefully. "Answer!"

Beatrice's body shook. "His name is . . . is . . . is . . ." And with a cry, she collapsed.

The audience was stunned, angry, upset. Just when they were about to learn who had committed the horrible slaying in their town, the clairvoyant had fainted.

Harry (1874–1926) and Beatrice (Bess) Houdini (1876–1943) in 1899. They married in 1894 when he was twenty and she was eighteen.

## A MAGICIAN IS BORN

Houdini the Great and Mademoiselle Beatrice weren't mediums. They couldn't contact the spirits or solve murders. They were young married entertainers, ages twenty-three and twenty-one, making a living by performing fake séances. Spiritualism, fortune-telling, and mind reading attracted people, and Harry and Bess Houdini gave audiences what they wanted.

Harry had begun his life as Erik Weisz, born on March 24, 1874, in Budapest, Hungary. His father was a rabbi who moved

Ehrich Weiss at age eight in 1882 when he lived in Wisconsin. He immigrated to the United States from Hungary with his family when he was four.

Ehrich Weiss wearing track medals when he was about sixteen. From an early age, he was athletic and agile. He joined a New York City athletic club when he was fifteen and specialized in cross-country running.

the family to the United States in 1878. When they entered the country at Castle Garden in New York City, immigration officers gave them all English variants of their names. Erik became Ehrich Weiss.

For a time, the family lived in Appleton, Wisconsin, where Rabbi Weiss had friends. Ehrich had five brothers and one sister, who was the youngest of the seven children. After several years in Wisconsin, the family moved to New York City where jobs were more plentiful. Later in life, Ehrich would say that he was born in Appleton, perhaps to make himself seem thoroughly American.

Ehrich worked at odd jobs to help support the family. At age seventeen, he decided that he wanted to be a professional magician, and he adopted the stage name "Harry Houdini." The name came from the famous French magician Jean Eugène Robert-Houdin, whose autobiography had inspired Ehrich to go on the stage.

In his early twenties, Harry and his new wife, Bess, performed magic in small traveling circuses and shows. Like many other conjurers in the late 1800s, they incorporated supernatural elements into their stage act, such as fortune-telling and mind reading.

At sixteen, Harry had realized for the first time that mediums could be fakes when he caught one cheating during a séance. Since then, he had learned how to do séance tricks from the 1891 book *Revelations of a Spirit Medium*. He also attended more séances and observed the mediums' methods.

As part of their act, Bess performed as Mademoiselle Beatrice, a clairvoyant, who behaved as if she had fallen into a trance. She impressed the audience by revealing secrets and answering messages sealed in envelopes. To do this, Bess used information that Harry dug up when they arrived in town.

Armed with a notebook, he visited the cemetery with a local resident, gathering facts about the community from the tombstones and his guide. He found out about people who regularly visited séances by referring to the Blue Book, a compilation of sitters' personal details shared by traveling mediums. When the Harry and Bess included the material in their act, the audience was amazed. How could they possibly know so much about the town?

Although these spiritualism-themed performances brought in more customers than their regular magic shows, Harry came to regret doing them. He realized how deeply his audiences believed in what they heard. Bess later recalled, "The people were so pitiable, so trustful. Our messages probably gave them comfort, but it was a false comfort at best." They eventually stopped presenting séances.

Their life of performing was difficult, and the couple didn't make much money. But Harry's career took off after he focused on his escape act, freeing himself from locked trunks, handcuffs, chains, ropes, straitjackets, and sealed safes. His athletic ability and strength were advantages.

By 1900, Harry was on his way to becoming an international star famous for his daring escapes. An exceptional self-promoter, he generated attention by performing death-defying stunts publicly where reporters and spectators could watch. Houdini soon stood out among his competitors for his escapes rather than for his magic tricks.

Harry Houdini became famous for his escapes from locked chains. This photograph is from 1905, when he was thirty-one.

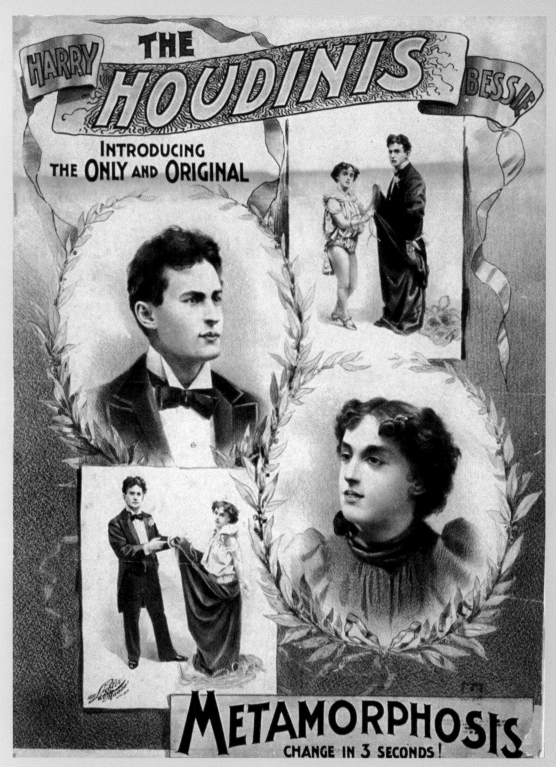

A poster from about 1896–97 advertises the Houdinis' early performance of Metamorphosis. In this illusion, Harry—with hands secured behind his back—is tied in a bag and locked in a box. A curtain is drawn around the box. Bess claps her hands three times and disappears behind the curtain. In three seconds, Harry reopens the curtain, having emerged from the bag and box with hands untied. When the box is opened, Bess is found inside the bag with her hands tied.

Houdini's Water Torture Cell (or Upside Down) was one of his most astounding escapes. He called it "the greatest sensational mystery ever attempted in this or any other age!!!," and he used posters like this (above left) to advertise.

This photograph from around 1913 shows how the act looked to an audience. Houdini hung upside down over a glass tank full of water with his ankles locked onto the tank's cover. After he was lowered headfirst into the water,

assistants fastened the cover in place and pulled a curtain around the tank.

As the minutes ticked by, the audience anxiously waited for Houdini to escape before he ran out of air. One of his assistants stood by with an ax, ready to break the glass in an emergency. Finally, after three tense minutes, Houdini jumped from behind the curtain, soaking wet.

To prepare for underwater feats, he practiced holding his

breath in the bathtub. His escapes and illusions were so incredible that many spiritualists believed he could dematerialize and pass through solid objects. Not true, said Houdini. "I do not *dematerialize* or *materialize* anything." His wife agreed. His tricks, she said, "were performed as the result of long forethought and skill, and persistent, arduous training, by a man of steel nerves, but there was no supernatural agency involved."

During his June 1914 return to New York after appearances in Europe, Houdini performed magic for passengers on the ocean liner. One member of his audience was former president Theodore Roosevelt (1858–1919). Houdini used a spirit slate to correctly answer Roosevelt's question for the ghosts: Where did I spend Christmas Day?

When the former president asked Houdini whether he had relied on spiritualism or magic to answer, the conjurer responded, "It is all hocus-pocus."

This photograph (top) was taken June 23, 1914, just a month before the outbreak of World War I. Houdini had the image altered so that when he displayed it, he appeared to be standing alone with the former president. The other five men were scratched or cropped out.

## MARVELS, WAR, DISEASE

By the start of the twentieth century, more than fifty years had passed since the Fox sisters sparked the worldwide interest in spiritualism. Publicized retractions, exposés, and investigations had thrown a negative light on the movement. Spiritualism's popularity had waned.

Still, true believers had new reasons to support their religion. The world was witnessing incredible scientific discoveries. Electricity flowed through wires to light up homes. Radio waves invisibly carried messages across thousands of miles. X-rays enabled doctors to see inside the body. Machines allowed humans to fly like birds.

These marvels seemed like magic. How they worked was a mystery to most people. Spiritualists argued: Why shouldn't we believe the equally marvelous fact that spirits are able to communicate with the living? Mediums allow spirits to be seen the way a light bulb allows invisible electricity to be seen.

The appeal of knowing the future or connecting with dead family and friends continued to attract people to mediums. But for many, spiritualism had become a form of entertainment rather than a religion.

All that changed in 1914.

During World War I, American soldiers are loaded into an ambulance at a field hospital in France. These patients had been gassed. Chemical weapons, including chlorine, phosgene, and mustard gas, were used by all sides as a weapon. The gasses blinded soldiers or burned their skin. When the gas was inhaled, the men suffocated. Although many soldiers eventually wore gas masks to protect themselves, some researchers estimate that these chemical weapons caused more than a million deaths or injuries.

For four years, from July 1914 to November 1918, the world was consumed by the Great War, now called World War I. The carnage was shocking. By the time the conflict ended, an estimated 15 to 22 million soldiers and civilians were dead. The United Kingdom alone lost about a million soldiers and civilians—2 percent of its population. At least one death occurred in nearly every British family. The United States entered the war in spring 1917, and about 117,000 of its soldiers died.

More death followed. In early 1918, an influenza pandemic broke out. Although exact numbers are unknown, researchers estimate that 50 million people died worldwide from the disease during its two-year run. Some think the total deaths reached 100 million. In the United States, about 675,000 died.

This widespread loss of life from war and disease brought devastating grief to families across the globe. Many turned to séances for comfort, hoping for a sign or a word from their dead loved ones. Mediums flourished. And by 1920, the numbers of spiritualists had swelled again.

In October 1918, these Red Cross workers in St. Louis, Missouri, hold stretchers ready to load influenza victims into ambulances. Historians estimate that one-third of the world's population—about 500 million people—were sickened by influenza from early 1918 to early 1920.

## THE SPIRITUALIST

Harry Houdini's successful career as an escape artist took him throughout the United States, Europe, and Australia, and it brought him wealth. He met presidents as well as acclaimed authors, stage performers, and actors. He starred in silent movies.

With his money, he was able to pursue his fascination with the history of conjuring and the occult. He began collecting tens of thousands of books, pamphlets, and other printed materials about magic and the supernatural as far back as 1489. Part of his collection covered spiritualism.

The Great War had prevented Houdini from touring foreign countries with his show. In early 1920, after the war ended, he once again traveled to England to perform. Always eager to promote himself, he sent out to prominent Britons about two hundred copies of his 1906 book, *The Unmasking of Robert-Houdin.*

One copy went to Sir Arthur Conan Doyle, the well-known author of the Sherlock Holmes stories. Conan Doyle wrote a letter to thank Houdini but also to comment about the Davenport brothers, whom Houdini had mentioned in the book. An ardent spiritualist, Conan Doyle questioned Houdini's statement that one of the brothers admitted their work was the result of rope escape skills, not spirit manifestations. Conan Doyle, like most spiritualists, considered the Davenports great mediums.

In July 1910, Houdini visited Ira Davenport, the surviving Davenport brother, at his home in western New York. Ira died a year later at age seventy-one.

Houdini didn't argue, even though when he visited Ira Davenport ten years before, the man had shown him how the brothers escaped from knotted ropes. Instead, Houdini told Conan Doyle "that the Davenport Brothers never were exposed."

Conan Doyle was interested in

Houdini's book collection and his knowledge of spiritualism. Houdini enjoyed associating with a famous author. The two men started a friendship, writing letters and occasionally meeting in person.

Houdini believed in an afterlife, but he was skeptical that the dead could communicate with the living. He wrote to Conan Doyle that although he had never seen a séance that wasn't faked, he was eager to visit any medium Conan Doyle suggested. "I promise to go there with my mind absolutely clear, and willing to believe."

Conan Doyle saw Houdini as a potential recruit to spiritualism. He gave his new friend the names of mediums who he thought were particularly gifted, including the woman who had spoken to him in the voice of his dead son.

# SIR ARTHUR CONAN DOYLE

Scottish-born Arthur Conan Doyle (1859–1930) was trained as a physician but gave up practicing medicine for his writing career. He was the author of the popular Sherlock Holmes detective stories, the first of which appeared in print in 1887. Conan Doyle also wrote other fiction, nonfiction, poetry, and plays. In 1902, he was knighted by the British king for his history of the Boer War in South Africa.

Conan Doyle became interested in spiritualism in 1886 after attending séances at an acquaintance's home.

**Arthur Conan Doyle at his desk a few years before meeting Harry Houdini in 1920**

He wasn't swayed by what he saw, but he was curious enough to study spiritualism further and attend other séances. In 1893, Conan Doyle joined the British Society for Psychical Research. Although the group exposed some dishonest mediums, Conan Doyle believed that what he witnessed at times was caused by supernatural forces.

When the Great War (World War I) broke out, Sir Arthur's belief in spiritualism grew stronger. His son Kingsley and five other close relatives died in the war and in the influenza pandemic that occurred during and after it. Conan Doyle attended numerous séances and claimed to have had several conversations with his son and with his brother who had both died from influenza.

Conan Doyle's wife also got involved in the religion when her brother was killed early in the war. She was convinced he visited her during a séance,

and she came to believe that she had the power of an automatic writing medium.

Because the couple found comfort and strength in spiritualism, Conan Doyle decided it was his duty to pass on his knowledge to others and bring more people to the religion. He became one of its leading champions, spreading the message that spiritualism was "the most important thing for two thousand years in the history of the world." He presented lectures around the world and wrote articles and books, including a two-volume history of spiritualism that celebrated its ideas and its most admired mediums. He endorsed spirit photography as proof of ghosts' existence.

Even after mediums and spirit photographers whom he praised were caught cheating, Conan Doyle refused to change his opinion about them or spiritualism. He explained to Houdini about one exposed medium: "She has her off-days, as every medium has."

Many people found it surprising that the creator of Sherlock Holmes—a detective who solved crimes with careful observation, scientific tools, and critical thinking—would ignore such strong evidence. Houdini commented about his friend: "In his great mind there is *no* doubt."

Conan Doyle died of a heart ailment at age seventy-one, ten years after he began his friendship with Harry Houdini.

An illustration by Sidney Paget (1860–1908) from Conan Doyle's 1892 Sherlock Holmes story, "The Adventure of Silver Blaze." Holmes (right) wears his famous deerstalker cap as he and his sidekick, Dr. John Watson, discuss a case in a train car. Paget's illustrations established Holmes's physical appearance for the public. Conan Doyle later said that Sherlock was more handsome in the illustrations than the man he had in mind when he wrote the stories. The author wrote fifty-six short stories and four novels about the detective.

On board an ocean liner in 1923, Sir Arthur Conan Doyle poses with his second wife, Jean (1874–1940), and their three children. He also had two children with his first wife, who died of tuberculosis in 1906. He remarried in 1907.

## ECTOPLASM

One medium on Conan Doyle's list was Marthe Béraud (called Eva C.), a French woman in her early thirties. When Eva was in a trance, ectoplasm oozed from her body. Spiritualists believed that ectoplasm was solid proof of a spirit world.

The appearance of ectoplasm had become the newest manifestation at séances. A French physiologist made up the term around 1894 after seeing material coming from a medium's body. He based the word on Greek: *ecto* for external and *plasm* for a substance shaped or formed. Depending on the observer, ectoplasm appeared as a vapor or a sticky solid resembling soft dough or netting. It was usually light-colored or luminous.

In a flashlight photograph of Eva C. during a séance in 1912 (left) and one of a Polish medium in 1913, the women exhibit ectoplasm apparently coming from their bodies. These photographs convinced spiritualists like Arthur Conan Doyle that ectoplasm was real.

Skeptical investigators found that ectoplasm was far from supernatural. When tested, it turned out to be chewed paper, gauze, cheesecloth, egg whites, or even animal parts. The spirit faces had been cut out from magazines and newspapers. Assistants often helped the medium pull off the deception.

The substance reportedly seeped from any opening in the medium's body, including the ears, mouth, and nose. Once outside, it often formed itself into the shape of an arm or face or a complete body. Spirits supposedly used ectoplasm to materialize and produce various phenomena at séances, such as rapping, moving objects, and touching sitters. At the end of the séance, the ectoplasm was reabsorbed into the medium's body.

The medium warned sitters that touching the ectoplasm could harm her. Because light interfered with the emergence of ectoplasm, séances had to be held in the dark. Skeptics pointed out that these rules prevented sitters from finding out exactly what ectoplasm was made from and where it originated.

Upon learning about Eva C., Houdini arranged to attend one of her London séances. Before it began, Eva was searched in an adjoining room by a woman sitter who looked for hidden substances. Eva dressed only in black tights to prove that she wasn't concealing anything under her clothes. A black net veil encircled her head to prevent her from putting items into her mouth.

As she took her seat with the visitors at a round table in the darkened séance room, the group joined hands. Houdini and the rest of the sitters waited while Eva's female companion put her into a trance.

Finally, after a long wait, Houdini spotted about 5 inches (12.7 cm) of luminous foam shoot from Eva's mouth and stick to the veil covering her face. Then a white patch appeared around her eye. To Houdini, the face on the patch looked like a colored cartoon.

Eva said that she felt something in her mouth. Could she use her hands to pull it out from under the veil? The group agreed. From her mouth, she extracted something wet. Houdini thought it resembled a piece of inflated rubber. No sooner had the sitters seen it than it disappeared.

Houdini wasn't impressed. The foam that oozed from Eva's mouth might have been soap lather hidden in her mouth or regurgitated from her stomach. He also recognized Eva's sleight of hand when she pulled the blob from her mouth. He suspected that she had actually put the "ectoplasm" *into* her mouth before announcing that it was between her fingers.

He had experience with similar tricks in concealing keys and lock picks and in performing his swallowing needles trick.

After several more séances with Eva, Houdini had no doubt that she was a fake. He didn't share his true opinion with Conan Doyle.

While Houdini was in England that year, he attended dozens of séances. He wasn't convinced by a single one.

Harry Houdini (right) poses with Sir Arthur Conan Doyle in London in 1920.

Houdini (left) knew something about regurgitation deceptions. In his Needle Trick, he put twenty-five or more sewing needles and a long piece of thread into his mouth and appeared to swallow them. Each needle was about 1.75 inches (4.45 cm) long. He invited audience members to come onstage and check his mouth to prove that the needles and thread weren't there. Then he dramatically "regurgitated," pulling out of his mouth the thread with all the needles now threaded and hanging from it. This photograph was a staged publicity shot.

## THE INEXPLICABLE TRICK

Houdini and Conan Doyle kept up their correspondence about spiritualism throughout the next two years.

In spring 1922, Conan Doyle, his wife, and three children sailed to the United States, where he gave a series of speeches promoting spiritualism. When the family came to New York City, Harry and Bess invited Sir Arthur and Lady Jean Conan Doyle to their home for lunch.

During the visit, Houdini took Conan Doyle to see the library in his house. The magician offered his British friend a demonstration.

Houdini picked up a slate that had holes bored into two of its corners. Threaded through the holes were wires with hooks on the ends. Houdini handed Conan Doyle the slate to examine. Then he asked Sir Arthur to hang the slate somewhere in the room using the wires and hooks so that it dangled without touching anything else. Sir Arthur attached the hooks to the edge of a picture frame and to a large book on a shelf.

Next Houdini produced four small cork balls in a saucer, a spoon, and an inkwell full of white ink. He told Sir Arthur to pick a ball, examine it, and cut it in half with a knife to verify that it was solid cork. Then, at Houdini's direction, Sir Arthur used the spoon to put one of the other balls in the white ink and stir until the ball was totally white.

Finally, Houdini asked Conan Doyle to go outside and walk away from the house in any direction that he wished. When he was alone, he was to write a phrase on a piece of paper before sticking it into his pocket. Then he was to walk back to the house.

After Sir Arthur returned to the library, Houdini asked him to use the spoon to remove the ink-soaked ball from the inkwell. With the white ball resting on the spoon, Sir Arthur was told to hold it next to the hanging slate. As soon as he did this, the ball mysteriously stuck to the slate and rolled across it, writing words. When it finished, the ball fell to the floor.

On the slate was an Old Testament phrase: "Mene, mene,

tekel, upharsin." It exactly matched the paper in Sir Arthur's pocket.

Conan Doyle was astonished. The writing must have appeared by a supernatural means. No, Houdini said, "I won't tell you how it was done, but I can assure you it was pure trickery."

Houdini implored his friend not to assume things were supernatural just because he had no other explanation. But it would take more than a magic trick to change Arthur Conan Doyle's view of spiritualism.

# HOW DID THEY DO IT?

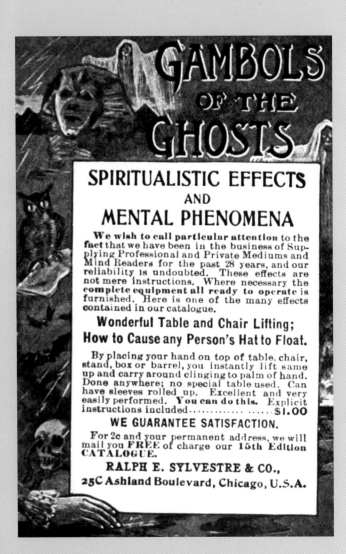

## SÉANCE MANIFESTATIONS

Although fraudulent mediums denied it, businesses supplied them with equipment that they used to cheat their customers during séances. The Sylvestre & Company of Chicago sold ghost hands and luminous spirit costumes in all sizes. A medium could buy spirit slates that wrote messages, tables that rapped, and chairs that lifted off the floor.

On sale was a lightweight telescopic reaching rod that could fit in the medium's pocket, extend to 6 feet (about 2 m), and pick up and carry an object such as a trumpet or guitar. A self-playing guitar was available, too. When a stuffed glove on the end of the rod touched a sitter's cheek, it felt like a ghost hand.

The owner of Martinka's Magic Shop in New York City sold equipment to professional magicians, and he was familiar with their tricks and illusions. Mediums were also Francis Martinka's customers. He provided items for séances, including extension rods, glow-in-the-dark paint, and other props. He once said, "Mediums are all fakers."

A 1901 advertisement for *Gambols of the Ghosts*, a catalog of equipment for mediums

68

## MIND READING AND FORTUNE-TELLING

Magicians had long incorporated mind reading into their acts. To pull this off, they used tricks, none of which involved a special power of telepathy.

Harry and Bess Houdini performed several mind reading tricks. In one, Bess went into the audience and asked someone to remove a dollar bill from his pocket. From the stage, Harry astounded the crowd by rattling off the bill's long serial number. He seemed to have supernatural abilities.

They did the trick by using a code in which a word stood for each number up to ten. For example, pray = 1, answer = 2, say = 3. While standing next to the dollar bill's owner, Bess kept talking to the audience. By incorporating the code words into her chatter, she told Harry the serial number.

Fake mediums promised séance visitors answers to their questions direct from the spirit world. As sitters entered the séance, they were given a slip of paper and an envelope and told to write down a question. People often wanted to know: Is my mother happy in the spirit world? Will I lose my job? Will I get married this year?

After the sitters wrote their question on the paper, they sealed the unfolded slip of paper inside the envelope and dropped it in a basket.

During the séance, the medium took one of the sealed envelopes from the basket. He held it to his head as if concentrating on its contents and receiving a message from the spirit world. He announced what the paper inside the envelope said and provided an answer to the question. When he finished, he tore open the envelope and read the question aloud to the group to verify how accurate he had been. Then he went on to another envelope in the basket.

How did mediums (and magicians) fool people? The key is for the medium (or magician) to find out what's written on the paper inside the envelope without letting on that he's done so. Next he comes up with an answer using details that he already

For a 1925 magazine article, Houdini demonstrates how a medium can produce spirit ectoplasm. A cloud of fine cloth netting comes from his mouth and drifts over his shoulder. Behind him in the dark is an assistant holding a luminous mask in the midst of the netting. In an unlit séance room, a sitter would not see the assistant dressed in black. Mediums concealed the "ectoplasm" up a sleeve, somewhere else in their clothing, or even in their body as Houdini did in this photograph.

knows about the sitter. If he doesn't have any personal information, he makes up a general, but convincing response.

One way to do this trick is the one-ahead method. Before the sitters see the medium take an envelope from the basket, he has already removed one (envelope #1) without the sitters noticing. He has opened it, quickly read and memorized the question, and put the envelope out of view.

What the sitters observe is the medium taking an envelope (#2) from the basket. (They assume it's the first one he has removed.) The medium holds the sealed envelope to his head, pretending to detect the question inside. But the answer he gives is to envelope #1's question, now hidden away.

The medium rips open envelope #2 and pretends to read the question, although he is actually quoting the question from envelope #1. Now he has seen the question from envelope #2. When he draws again from the basket (envelope #3), he will use the question from envelope #2. He is always one envelope and question ahead.

Another method for this psychic trick requires quick hands and a small sponge. The sponge, concealed in the medium's hand, is soaked in alcohol. As she picks up an envelope from the basket and calls to the spirits, she wets it with the alcohol. Everyone sees her hands, but she makes sure they don't spot the sponge.

When she presses the envelope to her forehead as if receiving the message, she reads the question through the wet envelope. Dramatically, she states the question to the sitters and invents a satisfying and impressive answer from the spirits.

Because alcohol evaporates quickly, the unopened envelope is dry and the writing hidden when the medium hands it back to the owner.

## THERE ARE NO SECRETS

People were amazed when mediums and fortune tellers seemed to know all about them. Often the medium really did know about them, but there was nothing supernatural about it.

After a customer called to make an appointment, the medium or her assistant investigated the person and gathered enough facts for an awe-inspiring séance.

Some fake mediums employed informants in the neighborhood who befriended people and steered them toward a séance. Before the sitters ever arrived, the informant had provided the medium with plenty of useful facts.

One successful medium owned a beauty shop where his wife and two daughters worked. They collected details about people in town from gossiping clients.

Fraudulent mediums kept track of newspaper death, marriage, and birth announcements in the area where they operated. They hired people who worked in local funeral homes to fill them in on grieving families.

When sitters arrived at a séance, they were ushered into a room to wait. From an adjoining room, the medium or assistant listened to conversations among the waiting group. People revealed facts about themselves while they chatted.

Assistants sometimes learned information by examining a sitter's coat hanging in the entryway. Did the person smoke? Did he carry a personal item with initials, such as a pen or lighter? Did the coat's labels give hints about where she bought it and how wealthy she was?

A medium who supposedly went into a trance gleaned information from unsuspecting sitters when they spoke or reacted during the séance.

Fake mediums were gifted at observation. They noticed clothing, jewelry, wedding rings, hair styles, and accents. They picked up other clues from the sitter's questions.

If these methods failed, mediums fished for details with vague statements. "I'm getting a message from . . . do you know a Jim or a John?" Watching the sitter's face, the medium knew when he got close.

All the collected clues about a person helped the medium or fortune teller make up believable predictions of the future or messages from the dead.

# CHAPTER SIX
## THE SPOOK HUNT

*"I do not say there is no such thing as spiritualism, but state that in the thirty years of my investigation nothing has caused me to change my mind."*
*—Harry Houdini, 1922*

Several weeks after Houdini dazzled Conan Doyle with his cork ball and slate trick, the two men, their wives, and the Conan Doyle children visited Atlantic City, New Jersey. On a June Sunday afternoon, Lady Conan Doyle offered to provide a special séance for Houdini. She felt that she might be able to bring him a message that day.

Before he left for the séance, Bess alerted her husband that the night before, she'd had a conversation with Lady Conan Doyle about his deceased mother. During their talk, Bess had discussed how much Harry loved his mother. She revealed a few of the private rituals they shared. Houdini was prepared for whatever might happen.

## A GHOSTLY MESSAGE

When Houdini reached the Conan Doyles' suite, Sir Arthur lowered the shades to darken the room. Then the three of them sat at a table already set up with pencils and a pad of paper.

Harry Houdini kisses his mother, Cecelia Weiss, on a street in Rochester, New York, in 1908. Houdini was devoted to his mother, who died in 1913 from a stroke. He hoped that he would communicate with her during a séance, but it never happened.

Sir Arthur bowed his head and uttered a prayer, asking for a sign from the spirit world. He laid his hands on his wife's.

Houdini tried to stay open-minded. He wanted nothing more than to communicate with his dead mother.

Lady Conan Doyle picked up a pencil. Soon her right hand jerked and beat the table, and her voice quivered as she asked the spirits for a message. With the pencil, she drew a cross at the top of the first sheet on the pad. Then she began to fill page after page with automatic writing, supposedly a message from Houdini's mother. When she reached the end of each sheet, Sir Arthur ripped the page from the pad and handed it to Houdini.

"Oh, my darling, thank God, thank God, at last I'm through," his mother's letter began. "I've tried, oh, so often—now I am happy."

The message continued with expressions of love for her son and assurance that she was content. "God bless you, too, Sir Arthur," the letter went on, "for what you are doing for us—for us, over here—who so need to get in touch with our beloved ones on the earth plane."

Houdini remained polite, but he knew his mother hadn't sent the message. She had been Jewish and wouldn't start her letter with a cross. And she wouldn't communicate with him in English because Cecelia Weiss barely spoke the language and never learned to write it.

Lady Conan Doyle didn't appear to be deliberately deceiving him. She seemed to believe the spirits were guiding her hand. Perhaps, Houdini thought, she subconsciously wrote what she presumed he'd want to hear.

Sometime later, he expressed his doubts about the message. Conan Doyle tried to explain that his mother had learned English in the afterlife because spirits became more educated there.

Houdini didn't buy it. Several months after Lady Conan Doyle's séance, he wrote a newspaper article stating that, though there might be such a thing as spiritualism, he'd never experienced anything to convince him of communication with the dead.

When Conan Doyle saw the article, he was upset that Houdini had insulted his wife's mediumship abilities by implying that she had faked the séance. He wrote Houdini, "I felt rather sore about it."

For his part, Houdini was offended that his love for his mother had been exploited. He wrote back that he knew the Conan Doyles treated spiritualism as a religion, but he couldn't do that. "Up to the present time, and with all my experiences, I have never seen or heard anything that could really convert me."

In Houdini's opinion, Conan Doyle's devotion to spiritualism was so strong that he was blind to any evidence that disproved it. The magician saw danger in such strong beliefs.

The two men never overcame this disagreement, and their warm friendship ended.

# SÉANCE STUDIES

Some scientists and other scholars believed that the scientific method could prove—or disprove—the existence of a world beyond what we experience with our five senses. Were the strange occurrences due to some outside force—the spirit world—or due to a medium's special ability?

In the late 1800s, organizations similar to the 1884 Seybert Commission were founded to study mediums, ghosts, haunted houses, and other phenomena. Two of these groups were the Society for Psychical Research in Britain and the American Society for Psychical Research.

Investigators used various techniques to test

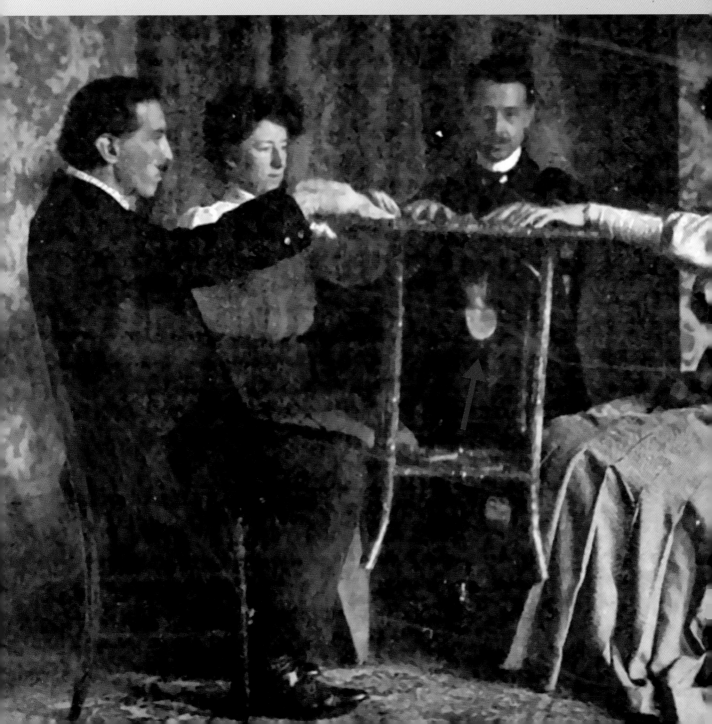

whether a medium was a fraud. They attended a séance with guests who gave assumed names so that the medium wouldn't have previous knowledge about them. Researchers hired detectives to follow the medium and learn whether she had informants who supplied material.

If the medium agreed—and many would not—the investigators imposed strict rules such as keeping hands atop the table. A few researchers insisted the lights stay on and set up cameras to film the action in the séance room. Others used magnets and electric wire to detect forces around the medium.

While researchers discovered that séances were often faked, mediums occasionally left them dumbfounded. Some investigators were convinced that these mediums must have supernatural powers. How else could a person possibly create the extraordinary spirit manifestations? How else could the medium know private details or read minds?

Other scientists were skeptical. An American psychologist wrote in 1895 that when a person couldn't figure out how something happened during a séance, he or she assumed that a medium had used mental telepathy or had spirit help. "It is quite possible," he wrote, "to invent half a dozen hypotheses which would equally well explain the facts."

Magicians were critical of the investigations, too.

British magician William Marriott began studying séance ghost appearances, spirit slates, and trance writing after many members of the British Psychical Research Society accepted the phenomena as proof of spiritualism. Marriott concluded, "As conjuring-tricks they are often fairly good, as evidence of a spirit world they are always miserably inadequate."

Houdini claimed that his many years as a conjurer allowed him to see trickery when scientists and other highly educated investigators could not. "I am not surprised such a large number of sensible people become convinced that they have had communication with the other world," he said in May 1922. "It is simply a case of matching expert wits against the untrained."

On this point, Conan Doyle once again disagreed with Houdini. He wrote, "Views of conjurers . . . are generally not only unintelligent, but quite spiteful about phenomena."

At a séance in 1910, British magician William Marriott (second from right) illustrates how fake mediums could raise a table using a foot (see arrow). The lights were on for the benefit of the camera. But during an actual séance, the room would be dark. Marriott attended hundreds of séances and didn't find a single phenomenon that he couldn't produce himself.

## THE PRIZE

Their differences put Houdini and Conan Doyle at odds again in early January 1923 when *Scientific American* magazine offered a prize to mediums who could prove they were genuine.

*Scientific American* had begun publishing in 1845 and was known for its articles about advancements in science and technology. The magazine noticed the widespread interest in spiritualism since the war. Arthur Conan Doyle's American lecture tour in 1922 had brought the subject additional attention.

The magazine's editors believed that existing data didn't prove one way or the other whether the claims of supernatural phenomena were true. To encourage more research, *Scientific American* pledged a prize of $2,500 (about $40,000 in today's money) for the first photograph that showed psychic phenomena and $2,500 to the first person who produced physical manifestations. Those could include sounds and sights created by a spirit. Mind reading and fortune-telling would not be eligible.

The magazine chose five judges who had experience studying the supernatural. The men brought different talents and training to the committee. Among the five were a physicist, a psychologist, a writer and amateur magician, and a psychic investigator. Houdini was asked to join, too, contributing his knowledge and experience as a professional magician.

Arthur Conan Doyle welcomed the investigation. But he warned *Scientific American* that the contest would draw out greedy fakers. "A large money reward will stir up every rascal in the country," he wrote in a letter to the editor, "while the best type of medium is unworldly and would not be attracted by such a consideration."

With the skeptical Houdini in mind, Conan Doyle advised that if the investigators don't attend séances with an attitude that is "gentle, quiet, courteous, sympathetic," they likely won't witness any psychic phenomena.

The judges set up scientific controls. In the tests, they used instruments such as microphones to record sounds in the séance room and a galvanometer to measure electric current changes. The medium's arms and legs were monitored or restrained to prevent cheating in the dark. If a medium used any apparatus, such as a slate, the Scientific American prize committee supplied it.

Spiritualists believed that spirits could leave proof of their ectoplasm in wax molds. Before a séance, a container was placed near the medium. It contained paraffin wax kept at its melting point by floating on warm water. During the séance, the spirit was asked to dip a hand into the melted wax two or three times. The wax coating hardened when the hand was immersed in a bowl of cold water. Throughout the séance, sitters heard water splashing in the dark.

When the spirit dematerialized and the lights came back on, an empty paraffin mold of the ghost's hand remained on the table. The medium argued that if a living person had made the mold, it would have broken when he removed his hand.

The wax mold could be filled with plaster of paris and later put in hot water to melt away the paraffin. That produced a cast of the spirit's hand for a grieving relative to cherish.

Image 1

Image 2

In these photographs, Houdini shows that spirit hands were created by humans, not ghosts. Demonstrating this technique, which had been around since the 1870s, Houdini dipped his hand into a container of melted paraffin, coating it up to the wrist (image 1). After he stuck his hand into cold water, the paraffin cooled and solidified (image 2). When the paraffin dried, he slowly and carefully removed his hand from the mold. In image 3, Houdini displays several spirit hands that he created.

A medium prepared the spirit hands ahead of time and hid them in a secret compartment in her chair, ready to place on the table in the darkness.

Houdini's demonstration did not change the views of most spiritualists, including Sir Arthur Conan Doyle.

Image 3

Mediums were slow to enter the contest. Of the few that did, the committee quickly determined that the entrants were using tricks to create manifestations.

In one test, the medium's chair was secretly rigged by the committee so that while he was seated, a light in the next room was on. But when he rose, the light went off. An assistant watching the bulb noted that every time it turned off, a manifestation occurred in the séance room. A trumpet played or a sitter felt a tap on the shoulder. That medium was eliminated as a contender for the prize.

In early 1924, the committee began testing a medium known as "Margery." She had drawn support from spiritualists and psychic investigators in England and America, including Arthur Conan Doyle. Her real name was Mina Crandon, and she was the third wife of Dr. Le Roi Goddard Crandon, a wealthy Boston surgeon and member of the Harvard University faculty.

Since 1923, Margery had been giving séances to small gatherings of the couple's friends in an upstairs room of their expensive Boston house on Lime Street. She didn't charge for her séances and didn't want the Scientific American prize money. The Crandons were more interested in recognition of Margery's talents.

In her séances, which usually occurred in the dark, Margery went into a trance. Soon the sitters heard a whistle, and a spirit voice came through. He identified himself as her older brother, Walter, who had been killed at age twenty-seven in a train accident when a railcar crushed him.

Walter spoke in a hoarse whisper and created noises in different parts of the room. According to reports from sitters, his ectoplasm emerged from Margery's body and took the form of an arm, leg, or hands. With it, Walter made lights float, furniture tilt and move, clocks start and stop. He took part in conversation around the séance table, and sitters found him witty and sassy.

## THE MARGERY BOX

Some members of the *Scientific American* committee had already attended dozens of séances with Margery before Houdini learned about them. When he heard that the judges were ready to present her with the prize, he made sure that he had the chance to

Mina Crandon (1890–1941), the medium called Margery, in 1924 at age thirty-four. Previously married and mother to a young son, Mina was seventeen years younger than her husband.

evaluate her immediately. In July 1924, he traveled to Boston.

During the tests before Houdini was included, the committee had set up a bell-box. Inside the wooden box was an electric bell connected to batteries. A lid was attached to the box with a spring. Whenever pressure was applied to the box lid, the bell rang.

Throughout the séances with Margery, the bell rang, sometimes producing a code to answer questions. She claimed that Walter had pressed the box top.

Houdini didn't think the conditions at these previous séances had been adequate to prevent cheating. Dr. Crandon, Margery's husband, always sat in the circle holding her right hand. That gave her the chance to use it in the dark when he let go. The judges believed they could detect motion of Margery's feet by resting their own legs against hers, but Houdini wondered whether she had outsmarted them.

He was also suspicious of J. Malcolm Bird, a *Scientific American* editor and the nonvoting secretary of the committee. Bird had been eager to grant Margery the prize even before Houdini tested her.

On July 24, 1924, Margery (Mina Crandon) posed outside her Boston home with Houdini (right), Orson Munn, publisher of *Scientific American* (left), and J. Malcolm Bird, an editor of the magazine and secretary of the investigating committee.

Houdini believed he was biased because he had stayed overnight at the Crandons' home numerous times and had become close to them. In Houdini's opinion, that was inappropriate. The investigating committee should remain impartial.

Houdini suspected that one of the judges, Hereward Carrington, might be helping Margery win the prize, too. Carrington had spent more than forty days and nights at the Crandons' Lime Street house. Whenever the rest of the committee had seen manifestations at Margery's séances, Carrington or Bird had been present.

Houdini prepared for his first sitting with Margery knowing that he would be holding her left hand and touching her left ankle with his foot. Throughout the day, he wore a rubber bandage around his right leg below the knee. By the time of the evening sitting, his lower leg was tender and painful, making it extremely sensitive. When he sat down in the circle, he pulled up his pant leg. That enabled him to feel any movement of Margery's left foot or leg muscles.

He placed the bell-box between his feet. As the séance continued in the dark, he felt Margery's ankle slowly moving until her foot touched the box top. Each time the bell rang, Houdini felt her leg flex.

In an illustration from Houdini's pamphlet exposing Margery, he shows how his sensitized right leg could detect the movement of her foot toward the bell-box between his feet.

FIG. 1.

At the next séance, he worked with *Scientific American*'s publisher, who sat next to him, so that Houdini could freely move his hand in the dark. When he did, he felt Margery's head tipping the table, an action the Crandons attributed to Walter.

But these discoveries weren't enough to convince the other judges that she was cheating. A month later, Houdini joined the committee to visit Margery again. For these tests, he had his assistant build a wooden cabinet that would prevent her from moving her torso and feet. The cabinet contained a seat and openings for her head and arms.

The bell-box was placed on a table in front of the cabinet.

This time Houdini and another committee member whom he trusted held Margery's hands—not her husband. Throughout the session, Walter insulted Houdini, and the bell rang.

Afterward, Houdini examined the cabinet. He realized that Margery had been able to push open the top and lean far enough forward to ring the bell with her head. The Crandons, however, said that Walter had opened the cabinet.

To strengthen the seal, Houdini's assistant added locks so that the lid could not be forced open. With Margery's legs, shoulders, and torso inside the cabinet, Houdini and a committee member held her hands.

The bell did not ring. Walter's ectoplasm had not been able to press the bell-box top.

Newspapers across the country picked up the story. One commented: "It seems that 'Margery,' highly successful spiritualistic medium of Boston, could not do 'her stuff' in a special locked box arranged by Houdini, the magician. . . . The radio or telephone would have worked in Houdini's box. The spirits are more sensitive."

In explaining the séance, Margery told a reporter, "There is no assurance that ectoplasm can be made to work through oak an inch thick."

Despite Margery's excuse, Houdini knew the real reason the bell was silent was that the secure wood cabinet prevented her from cheating.

As part of his investigation of Mina Crandon, Houdini created this contraption, which he called the Margery Box, to limit her movement during a séance. The first time he used it, Margery was able to push open the top and reach her body far enough to touch the box-bell, as demonstrated in the top image. For the second test, Houdini added more fasteners and covers for the arm holes to prevent that. The bell failed to ring.

## THE VOTE

In November, Houdini released a pamphlet exposing Margery as a fake and explaining how she did her séance tricks. He declared her undeserving of the Scientific American prize. But the committee had yet to vote, and Houdini was criticized for going public beforehand.

When *Scientific American* dragged its feet in announcing a decision about Margery, Houdini took matters into his own hands. He arranged for a demonstration at Boston's Symphony Hall in early January 1925, inviting Margery to participate. He challenged her to appear before a jury of journalists, magicians,

POSITIVE AND NEGATIVE PROOFS RESULT FROM PSYCHIC TESTS

"Margery" Demonstrates Power in One Box; Fails in Device Offered by Houdini—Judges Disagree; One Quits Board.

A headline from the *Evening Star*, a Washington, DC, newspaper on August 28, 1924. The press followed the drama surrounding Houdini and Margery.

rabbis, and priests and produce a manifestation that he couldn't replicate. If she didn't accept, he would provide the audience with an exposé of all her methods.

Margery didn't show up. Houdini put on a two-hour show in full light before a crowded auditorium. He demonstrated the tricks she used during the *Scientific American* tests as well as some of his own.

Dr. Crandon was furious. He charged that Houdini was ignorant about psychics and "came with his mind made up before he started." Privately, Crandon made anti-Semitic comments about the magician. In a letter to Arthur Conan Doyle, he wrote that he was sorry "this low-minded Jew has any claim on the word American." During one of Margery's séances, Walter sang an anti-Semitic song about Houdini.

Eventually, Crandon refused to continue with the *Scientific American* committee's tests of his wife, saying that she couldn't prove herself under the conditions they imposed.

In its April 1925 issue, the magazine announced that "the famous Margery case is over so far as the Scientific American Psychic Investigation is concerned. . . . The psychic award will not be granted to 'Margery.'"

Of the five voting judges, four said that, despite many hours of observation and several séance sittings, everything they saw could have been produced in a nonsupernatural way. They couldn't prove that Margery *never* produced ectoplasm, though it hadn't happened in their presence.

In his official statement printed in the magazine, Houdini reported that he'd seen Margery use her head, shoulders, and left foot in creating manifestations. "Everything which took place at the seances which I attended was a deliberate and conscious fraud." Margery was cunning and knew how to use conjuring tricks, but she wasn't an authentic medium. If she had psychic power, he didn't witness it.

Only one of the committee members voted in favor of giving Margery the prize. Hereward Carrington said, "I am convinced that genuine phenomena have occurred here."

No other mediums impressed the judges, and the Scientific American prize was never awarded.

## MORE INVESTIGATIONS

Margery continued to hold séances. Undeterred by the *Scientific American* report, people from around the world visited Lime Steet.

Over the next few years, Dr. Crandon allowed other researchers to test his wife. Like the *Scientific American* committee, they weren't won over. Investigators complained that their work had been hampered by the Crandons' rules, allegedly coming from Walter. They were forbidden to use light at séances, to examine the ectoplasm, or to control where and when séances were held.

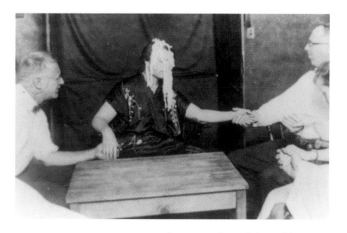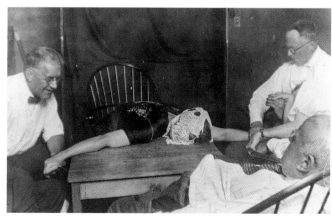

In photographs exhibited by Dr. Crandon in 1925, ectoplasm appears to leave Margery's ears and spread around her head until she collapses. Crandon said that as soon as ectoplasm was exposed to the flash for the photograph, it shrank and disappeared.

Despite those restrictions, researchers caught Margery taking objects from under her robe and moving them around on the table. They saw her using her foot to ring the bell-box. Harvard scientists identified the ectoplasm that supposedly emerged from her body as part of an animal's windpipe and lung.

During her séances, Margery revealed a thumbprint in dental wax that she said was made by Walter. But an investigator discovered that the print was actually from her dentist, a friend who had attended her séances. The man wasn't dead.

These exposures persuaded many of her earlier supporters that she was a fake. But Margery maintained the backing of others, including Arthur Conan Doyle who praised her as a gifted medium in his 1926 history of spiritualism. In the same book, Conan Doyle criticized Houdini for "his preposterous and ignorant theories of fraud" about her. After Conan Doyle's death in 1930, sitters at Margery's séances reported that his spirit showed up to offer advice.

Throughout Margery's career, several investigators, including Houdini, had reported her attempts to seduce them. She sometimes was successful. Years after the *Scientific American* tests, committee members Carrington and Bird admitted to having love affairs with her at the time of the contest.

Mina Crandon was a charming, attractive young woman who often hosted her séances wearing alluring clothing, such as slinky robes. Investigating committees were almost always comprised solely of men. A magician like Houdini recognized that she used her physical appearance as a form of misdirection, preventing sitters from noticing her tricks.

Margery was only one example of the deceptive mediums Houdini had seen since 1920. In an interview, he told a reporter, "Most people who go to a séance want to believe, or they are fascinated with the possibility that unearthly things are about to be revealed." But too many of them depended on a medium to solve all their problems, he said. That kept the frauds in business.

Houdini was more determined than ever to alert the world to these cheats.

Mina Crandon, "Margery," around the time of the 1924 *Scientific American* contest. Dr. Crandon died of pneumonia in late 1939 after falling and breaking his pelvis at their house. Margery continued holding séances for a while after his death. In November 1941, a few weeks before the United States entered World War II, she died of cirrhosis of the liver caused by her excessive drinking throughout the years. She was buried, not with her husband, but with her parents and older brother (the séance spirit Walter).

# CHAPTER SEVEN

## UNDERCOVER AGENTS

*"I do believe it is my duty, for the betterment of humanity, to place frankly before the public the results of my long investigation of Spiritualism."*
*—Harry Houdini, 1924*

In a small Nebraska farming town in 1923, a seven-year-old boy grieved for his mother who had recently died. He constantly asked his father, "Where is mamma?"

Herman Light assured his son, "Mamma's in another world, where we will soon be with her again."

Light had been involved in a local spiritualism group for several years, and he believed that the family would be reunited in death. After his wife died, Light had spent even more time studying spiritualism. He became increasingly depressed.

"We will soon see mamma," he told his son one April day.

A week later, father and son were found in convulsions on the floor of their home. Herman had given his son a drink laced with poison and then drank some himself. Both died.

The day of the funeral, Herman's best friend and fellow spiritualist shot himself. He left a suicide note saying that he longed to join his "friend Light in the great beyond, where all is peaceful and happy."

## RAISING THE ALARM

This story was among the newspaper clippings that Harry Houdini collected. He was troubled by tragedies involving people who had been taken in by spiritualist ideas.

One San Francisco man killed his two young sons after believing that his dead wife asked him to send their children to her. Houdini heard of another man who divorced his wife because she was in love with a spirit. Some victims had committed suicide, convinced they were headed to happiness with their dead loved one.

These stories motivated Houdini to do more to educate the public about what went on at séances. He had seen for himself that people who suffered intense grief or had troubled lives often weren't able to think critically. Searching for solace, they grabbed onto the smallest sign that a spirit was communicating with them. Because they thought a medium had special powers, they unquestioningly accepted all advice from the spirit world. As a result, many distressed people had been led to make terrible decisions.

Houdini's experience with spiritualists had convinced him that there were only two types: "tricksters and the deluded persons upon whom they prey."

In articles, books, lectures, and newspaper interviews, Houdini warned how fake mediums and fortune tellers gradually gained a person's trust by claiming to create supernatural phenomena. He revealed the tricks that these con artists used to materialize ghosts, bring messages from dead loved ones, or predict the future.

Houdini assisted New York City police in identifying the fraudsters who charged for bogus séances and readings or who persuaded a person to hand over money, sometimes a life's savings. He lectured at the police academy and shared tips for exposing the spook crooks so that they could be arrested. He even staged a séance to demonstrate the mediums' tricks. His séance, however, was in full light, not in the dark as a medium's séance would be.

In this 1924 magazine, Houdini published an exposé about a fraudulent medium he investigated. The cover depicts a female sitter embracing the man she believes is the spirit of her dead fiancé. After Houdini and his friend used a flashlight and cut off the ghost's escape from the room, the woman and the other sitters realized the spirit was the medium's assistant.

Houdini, seated on left, demonstrates how a medium is able to slip off his shoe even when the sitter has his foot placed on it. With his bare foot, Houdini rings a bell. The sitter assumes a spirit has done this because Houdini's hands and feet are held. Houdini trained himself to use his toes to write on a spirit slate, shake a tambourine, pinch a sitter's knee, and do other séance tricks.

Houdini wasn't the only one raising the alarm in the 1920s. Americans Joseph Rinn, Joseph Dunninger, and Julien Proskauer were three of Houdini's magician friends who publicly spoke and wrote about the deceptions of fake mediums.

In Buffalo, New York, a Jesuit priest gave talks about spiritualism, performing some of the mediums' tricks. "Even the best demonstrations of the mediums are but child's play for an adept mind-reader or magician," he told audiences. As an amateur conjurer, he was surprised that psychic researchers didn't realize that they were being fooled. "The higher these men go in the realm of science, the harder they fall for the wily medium," he said.

## FIGHTING THE FRAUDS

In 1924, Houdini expanded his campaign. He set out on a national lecture tour, appearing in theaters, universities, and churches. He illustrated his presentations with about fifty slide pictures covering the history of spiritualism. Included were images of the Fox sisters and the Davenport brothers with their famous cabinet.

Houdini told how he detected the fraud practiced by famous mediums such as Margery. One of his stories was about Lady Conan Doyle's supposed spirit message from his mother. He demonstrated the paraffin hands and other séance deceptions.

The next year, Houdini put together an expanded stage show. For part of the program, he performed escapes, tricks, and illusions including the Water Torture Cell, the Needle Trick, and Metamorphosis. Bess joined him as an onstage assistant.

Houdini's programs exposing mediums were popular among all age groups. These children wait in a theater's lobby ahead of one of his shows in 1925 or 1926.

The last portion was the spirit-exposure, designed to put the fakers out of business and warn people about their scams. In each city, Houdini announced the names of local mediums and presented the methods they used to swindle sitters.

Some indignant mediums filed lawsuits against him, which brought more headlines and free advertising for Houdini's show. Because of these lawsuits, Houdini had a secretary take notes as a record of everything he said on stage and in his speeches and interviews.

Although Houdini visited suspected fake mediums himself, his fame had made him easy to recognize. The medium community was aware that he was searching for frauds. To solve the problem, Houdini sent out others to séances. At first he relied on stage assistants, close friends, and family, including Bess and his niece Julia Sawyer.

Houdini's face was known so well that he had to disguise himself at séances when he was exposing fraudulent mediums. Here he pretends to be an old deaf man desperate to speak to his dead son's spirit.

This photograph was part of Houdini's 1925 article in *Popular Science Monthly* about spirit fakers. In the article, he wrote that whenever a medium was caught cheating, the spiritualists had a ready excuse: the medium had temporarily lost her power and was under such pressure to perform that she used tricks.

But with his traveling show stopping at so many different cities, he needed full-time investigators to supply enough information about local mediums. Finally, he hired twenty undercover agents. Though some were men, the majority were women. Houdini found that female agents were less likely to arouse suspicion among mediums. One of those women became his chief investigator.

## THE SPOOK SNOOP

Rose Mackenberg was born in New York City in 1892. Her parents had immigrated to the United States from Russia in the late 1880s. They were part of the wave of Russian Jews who left for America under the cloud of poverty, starvation, and persecution by the czar.

Rose Mackenberg (1892–1968), in her thirties

While living in Brooklyn with her parents and siblings, Mackenberg began working in her late teens as a stenographer in a law office. Later she took a job as an investigator at a New York City detective agency.

One evening when Mackenberg was off duty, a friend suggested they attend a séance for fun. Mackenberg agreed to go because she thought ghosts probably existed.

After paying their admission, they found the medium Myra sitting in front of a curtained area of the séance room. Myra allowed herself to be tied up to ensure that she didn't cheat in creating manifestations. Next, her assistant darkened the room. Within moments, the sitters heard brass and reed instruments playing. The spirits were there, Myra told them. It was too dark for Mackenberg to see otherwise.

Then Myra asked her assistant to turn the lights back on. The bass drum behind her, in full view of the sitters, suddenly pounded with a steady beat. The sitters were amazed. They could see that no one stood anywhere near the drum. Myra was bound. They readily believed her when she said the spirits were responsible. Mackenberg's friend was impressed.

But the private detective was suspicious. Mackenberg returned several nights later to get another look. This time she wore glasses and dressed like an older woman so that Myra wouldn't recognize her.

As soon as the lights went out, Mackenberg quietly slipped behind Myra's back. Reaching out her hand, she felt around the bass drum. To her surprise, her fingers touched a person curled inside. She had discovered Myra's spirit. The exceptionally small man played the instruments in the dark. When the lights went back on, he hid in the drum and thumped it.

Mackenberg didn't reveal her find to the other sitters that night, but she warned her friends about Myra so that they didn't waste their money on her séances. Mackenberg realized that the medium had certain traits that helped her deceive sitters. She was smart, beautiful, and charismatic. Her customers wanted to trust her. Mackenberg eventually heard that Myra left the medium business after a public exposure forced her to admit her fakery.

Sometime later, private detective Mackenberg was assigned a case that involved another fraudulent medium. Her client had been tricked into using his employer's money in a business deal. Mackenberg's job was to expose the medium who ran the scam and bring her to justice.

It was a tough assignment, and Mackenberg needed help. A friend introduced her to Harry Houdini. When she asked him for tips to catch the medium, he was glad to provide them.

After she cracked the case, Houdini was impressed by what he saw and heard about her. He offered to hire Mackenberg as one of his undercover agents. She wasn't sure she should accept. After all, she believed in ghosts. Houdini told her the position would be an ideal opportunity to find a genuine medium. She decided to give it a try.

Before she met Houdini, Mackenberg solved a case in which the medium (the woman tied to a chair) used an abnormally small man concealed in a drum to create ghostly sounds at a séance. Mackenberg's detective work impressed Houdini so much that he hired her.

## SETTING A TRAP

When Mackenberg came on board, Houdini taught her the tricks that fake mediums used. She learned that what people think they hear and see can be completely different from what really happens.

In one lesson, he showed her the way darkness allows mediums to fool sitters about where a sound originates. He blindfolded her and then clicked two coins together. Where was the sound coming from? Mackenberg thought he was standing in the corner across the room. She was astonished to learn that he had been holding the coins above her head. Her sense of direction had been confused in the dark.

Houdini sent Mackenberg to help undercover police officers who attended séances of suspected fraudsters. In the middle of one session, she turned a flashlight on a medium who was using a small megaphone to create ghostly voices. The officers made the arrest, and Mackenberg testified in court as a witness to the crime.

In the fall of 1925, one of her assignments for Houdini took her to the spiritualist community of Lily Dale. The village in western New York was a destination for visitors from all over the world seeking sittings with mediums. At one end of town stood the farmhouse in which the Fox sisters began their rapping. The house, revered by spiritualists, had been moved around 1916 from its original site in Hydesville.

Houdini was out to expose the medium Pierre Keeler, who he knew was operating in Lily Dale. In 1885, Keeler had been tested and dismissed as a fraud by the Seybert Commission. At that time, his séances featured a jangling tambourine, beating drum, strumming guitar, and ringing bells—all supposedly played by the spirits. Later Keeler moved on to spirit slates. In 1907, Hereward Carrington, who would become one of the *Scientific American* judges in 1923, caught Keeler cheating by switching slates. Now at the age of seventy, Keeler was still deceiving his clients.

Using the name Ethel Lockwood, Rose Mackenberg pretended to be a grieving widow. After paying $3 (about $50 today) for a sitting, she asked the white-haired Keeler to bring her word from her husband, her child, and eight of her friends. In truth, Mackenberg never married or had children, and she gave names of living or made-up friends. Keeler produced messages from each spirit anyway.

Later Mackenberg returned to Keeler's home with a girl who she said was her daughter. Julia Lockwood was actually Julia Sawyer, Houdini's niece. Although she was in her early twenties, Julia looked young enough to pass as a fifteen-year-old.

Julia paid her $3 and asked for a message from her dead sister. Keeler produced a slate message: "Dear Julie, Dear Mamma: I am happy. I have all I want. Papa got me two new skates. I have fun. I am your best girl and sister. Evelyn."

After their séance ended, the two women convinced Keeler to walk down the street to meet their wealthy uncle who had come to Lily Dale for a sitting. They found him in a wheelchair, pushed by a male nurse.

When Keeler approached, the uncle jumped from his wheelchair. He accused the medium of taking cash from widows and orphans and deceiving them with fake ghost messages. "I've tried to get you for a long time, Keeler," he said, pulling off his tinted glasses, "and now I've got you 100 per cent. I am Houdini."

## HOUDINI TRAPS MASTER MEDIUM

Houdini (right) is pictured with Pierre Keeler, the famous medium he exposed in 1925 at the spiritualist retreat of Lily Dale, New York. Helping him in the exposure was Rose Mackenberg (bottom left), bottom left, and Julia Sawyer, Houdini's niece. An article about the exposure was written by a newspaper reporter disguised as Houdini's male nurse. Newspapers in various parts of the country carried the story. This one was from Iowa.

Keeler knew he'd been caught. "I never would try to put over any spirit messages on you. After all, Houdini, we are all in the same business."

No, replied Houdini, they weren't in the same business. He was an entertainer, and audiences were aware of that when they came to see him. He didn't cheat people the way Keeler did.

Houdini had two witnesses to the séance, and he'd brought along a reporter—the nurse—to record Keeler's confession. But Houdini didn't stop at that. The reporter's account appeared in newspapers across the country. And in his stage show that week, Houdini recounted how he and his secret squad had caught Keeler.

## STAGE EXPOSURES

To prepare for his traveling program, Houdini sent his undercover agents to each city ten days before he was to take the stage. The investigators identified the local mediums by talking to residents and checking out newspaper advertisements.

Each agent stayed at a separate hotel to avoid being seen together, and everyone had an alias. Mackenberg used several spook-chaser names, including Ruth Masch, Allicia Bunck (All is a Bunck), and Frances Raud (F. Raud).

To gather the disguises she planned to wear when meeting mediums, Mackenberg dropped by a department store and noted what local women wore. She wanted to look as if she lived there. Among her characters were the frumpy housewife, the old woman with a hearing aid, and the mourning widow dressed in black.

When she attended a séance, Mackenberg invented a story about herself. She asked the medium to reach her husband or a dead child. During her investigations, she received spirit messages from dozens of husbands and children.

At some point while she was in the medium's house, she left her initials in chalk or crayon behind a mirror or painting frame. That proved that she'd been there in case the medium denied it.

Back at her hotel, Mackenberg wrote a report for Houdini. Besides the time and date of her visit, she included the layout of the séance room and the location of her hidden mark. Her report listed the medium's specialty, such as ectoplasm, mind reading, trumpet-speaking. She told Houdini the questions she had asked, the responses provided by the medium, and the tricks used.

During his show, Houdini named the mediums his agents had visited. He told the audience how these mediums defrauded their customers. Then he demonstrated their methods.

Mediums often came to his show, perhaps out of curiosity, feeling confident that they hadn't been found out. Using his agents' physical descriptions, Houdini picked out mediums in the audience and shined a flashlight on them.

Frequently when mediums were identified and their tricks exposed, they called out an objection. "That's a lie, an infamous lie!"

Houdini's undercover agent stepped onto the stage and related what had happened at the séance, giving details about the house and the hidden mark. That usually sent the medium scurrying from the theater.

Mackenberg's work was exhausting. Sometimes she had to call on fifteen to twenty mediums a day. It could be dangerous, too. Male mediums occasionally said they needed to touch her to get the right connection to the spirits. Or in the dark, they groped her. Mediums even attacked her, ripping at her clothing as she fought her way out of the séance room.

When she reported these men to the police, the mediums always denied her accusation. Mackenberg suspected other women were too embarrassed to go to the police. To catch the offenders, female police officers posed as vulnerable sitters.

After Houdini heard about these incidents, he urged Mackenberg to conceal a gun for her own protection. But she felt uncomfortable carrying one. Instead, she relied on her physical strength and wits to stay safe.

Mackenberg wore numerous disguises in her visits to mediums. In this one, she posed as an unmarried woman desperate for romance.

## THE $10,000 OFFER

In his shows and writing, Houdini went out of his way not to attack the religion of spiritualism. He also said he had no problem with people who wanted to hold a séance as entertainment for their friends. He made clear that his goal was to expose the deceptions of fraudulent professional mediums. If any genuine medium could create a spirit manifestation that he was unable to imitate, Houdini promised a prize of $10,000 (more than $150,000 today).

# The Church of the Religion of Love
and  of
# Spiritualistic Phenomena

אדני

צבאות

יהוה

Founded at
Atlantic City, New Jersey

January 25th, 1913
Incorporated February 4th, 1920

ישוע המשיח

**Certifies that** *Rev. Allicia Bunck of Philadelphia State of Pennsylvania* ~~~~~~ **Being duly ordained**

as a minister of Truth, Love and Light by our Divine Prophet-Priest

## G. Mahmud Ahmad Abdoullah

is authorized to hold Divine Spiritualistic meetings under the above name, being subject to the Constitution and By-Laws of said Religious Society, as a member of the Mother Church at Atlantic City, New Jersey.

Our Ministry consists of voicing, healing, helping, revealing, teaching comforting and making Peace by the Power, the Truth, the Love and the Light of the Spirit of God and of the Angel World.

**Signed** *G. M. A. Abdoullah*

מלכי-צדק מלך-שלם ברו לאל עליון קנה-שמים וארץ

Matt. 10: 5 to 42

Luke 10: 19, 20

Mark 16: 15 to 18

John 14: 12

Believe on the Seventeenth Chapter of the Gospel of St. John.

Believe also on the Book of Peace or Bible of the Easly Student.

To get around laws against defrauding people, mediums set up spiritualist churches. This protected them under the US Constitution's First Amendment, which provides freedom of religion. They didn't charge for sittings at the church because that would attract the attention of the police. But they surreptitiously passed out cards for private, paid sittings to those who were interested.

Someone who wanted to enter the medium business could pay these churches to be ordained as a minister and be granted a certificate like this one. Rose Mackenberg collected these, paying from $5 to $25 a piece (about $80 and $400 today). She had so many that her fellow undercover agents called her "the Rev" [Reverend]. Her other nickname was "Mac." This certificate was granted to Allicia Bunck [All is a Bunk], one of Mackenberg's aliases.

In September 1925, a woman accepted the challenge. Dr. Alice Dooley, pastor of the Pittsburgh [PA] Church of Divine Healing, agreed to go on stage with Houdini. She announced that she wanted to prove that some mediums were honest and authentic.

Under the conditions of the test, she agreed to use her spiritual powers to answer three of Houdini's written questions. Each was sealed in its own envelope. Dr. Dooley was not allowed to touch them.

She pointed to the first envelope and gave her answer for its question: "Not quite clear, but possibly March 30, 1864."

A committee of judges from the audience opened the envelope. One read the question: "What was the name of the first chief of police from Pittsburgh, whom I met in Europe?"

Her answer to the second was: "Is it possible?" The question was: "Who taught me the East Indian [Needle] trick?"

After failing on the first two questions, Dooley didn't try the third.

A woman in the audience screamed a curse at Houdini. The rest of the crowd joined in, yelling their opinions supporting or condemning him. His $10,000 prize went unclaimed that night. In fact, no one ever successfully met his challenge.

Houdini's program brought out strong emotions. Spiritualists were angry that he was attacking their religion, even though he argued that he wasn't. The spook crooks were upset that he was ruining their business.

At some of his shows, verbal fights broke out in the audience between spiritualists, fraudsters, and nonbelievers after Houdini exposed a medium. On occasion, these factions took their dispute outside the theater. Punches were thrown. Mackenberg was once caught up in a brawl and came out of it with a bruised ankle. Another Houdini agent had his coat torn off.

Houdini insisted that his mind was open about spiritualism. But he said that in all the séances he attended, he had yet to see "anything which has convinced me that it is possible to communicate with those who have passed out of this life."

He and several friends had promised each other that, if they were able, they'd make contact from the afterlife. After twenty-five years, Houdini told a journalist, "I have never received a word. . . . I am certain that if any one of those persons could have reached me he would have done so."

# HOUDINI AND SPIRIT PHOTOGRAPHY

Spiritualists claimed that the camera caught the image of ectoplasm in a spirit photograph. In May 1923, Houdini visited a spirit photographer whom Conan Doyle had recommended in Denver, Colorado, asking him to create a portrait.

The spirits circling his head include President Theodore Roosevelt on the left. (Roosevelt died in 1919.) Houdini had no doubt that these were cut-out pictures and that the photograph had been created using a double exposure technique. "With Spirit photography as with all other so-called psychic marvels," he said, "there never has been, nor is now, any proof of genuineness beyond the claim made by the medium."

To show how easy it was to produce a spirit photograph, Houdini paid another photographer to create an image of Abraham Lincoln sitting across from him. In February 1924, he sent a copy of it to a Lincoln relative, Mary Edwards Lincoln Brown, telling her that it wasn't a real spirit photograph, although some people claimed it was.

This image was included in the slideshow Houdini presented to his lecture tour audiences. Other slides pictured him standing next to celebrities such as Theodore Roosevelt, Harry Kellar, and Arthur Conan Doyle. Unlike Lincoln, they all were alive when Houdini posed with them.

## CHAPTER EIGHT
# CAPITAL SPIRITS

"Do not forget that extraoridinary things require extraordinary proof."
—*Harry Houdini, 1926*

On Friday morning, February 26, 1926, Harry Houdini faced a group of congressmen in a hearing room of the House of Representatives. "Washington is the only place where you can buy a license for $25 with which to blackmail and rob the public," he told the lawmakers.

Houdini was there as part of his campaign to prevent fraudulent mediums from cheating people. He had worked with two lawmakers from New York, Senator Royal Copeland and Representative Sol Bloom, who cosponsored a bill outlawing fortune tellers, clairvoyants, and fake mediums in Washington, DC.

While many states arrested mediums and fortune tellers when they swindled someone, Washington licensed and allowed these businesses. The Copeland-Bloom bill would make the activities punishable by a fine up to $250 (about $4,000 today) or six months in jail. The bill was proposed in the US Congress because the Constitution gave that body jurisdiction over Washington, the federal capital.

Houdini was invited to testify before members of both the

Harry Houdini leaves the Capitol in early 1926 after testifying for passage of the Copeland-Bloom bill.

Senate and the House of Representatives as they held hearings to collect information about the bill. His first appearance on February 26 was publicly announced the week before.

Washington's spiritualist and fortune-telling communities mobilized. Houdini was an unpopular figure among these people, and the bill threatened their livelihood. When Houdini testified that February day, dozens showed up to protest. The room was so crowded that many spectators couldn't get inside.

When it was his turn to speak, Houdini said, "I have examined 300 mediums, and this town is the worst I have ever struck. . . . They have not got one genuine medium in Washington." He charged that the swindlers were making large amounts of money off an unsuspecting public. The bill would stop that.

His statement infuriated some in the audience who resented being accused of cheating clients. Several women jumped up and shouted at him. One was Jane Coates, head of the Spiritual Science Church. Another was Grace Champney Marcia

# SPIRITUALISTS IN CLASH OVER BILL WITH MAGICIAN

### Houdini Declares He Never Met Medium Who Wasn't A Faker

The nation's newspapers carried stories about Houdini's appearance before the congressional committee. This is from the *Richmond* [IN] *Item*, February 17, 1926.

(known as Madame Marcia), an astrologer who claimed she had predicted the August 1923 death of President Warren Harding.

Three more hearings were scheduled for May. Houdini planned to be there.

## WHITE HOUSE SÉANCES

Ahead of those hearings, Houdini sent Rose Mackenberg to Washington to gather information about the city's mediums and fortune tellers. As she rode the train toward the capital, she prepared herself for the storm that was sure to occur at the hearing. Mackenberg had seen how mediums and spiritualists reacted to being exposed.

When she arrived, Mackenberg visited ten mediums. Houdini asked her specifically to check out Jane Coates and Madame Grace Marcia, who had spoken against the bill at the February hearing. Each woman had many clients, some of whom were important members of the city.

Mackenberg used the same techniques she always did when scouting out séances and mediums. She put together an alias, a disguise, and a false personal story. After her visit, she wrote a detailed report, including what her target had said to her.

*How Miss Mackenberg Used to Dress to Consult Mediums*

...tic Schoolteacher.    As a Small Town Matron.    As a Credulous Servant Girl.    As a "Believing" Semi-Invalid.    As a Woman Seeking Lost Relatives.    As a "Vamp" from the Country.    As a Tipsy Consultant.

Photographs of Mackenberg's many disguises. She used costumes and aliases to mislead mediums and hide her identify.

On Tuesday, May 18, 1926, with her assignment completed, Mackenberg sat down next to Houdini in a hearing room at the US Capitol. He would be the main witness that day, arguing for the bill's passage.

Like the February hearing, the room was packed with more than a hundred spectators, including mediums and spiritualists. Mackenberg spotted Coates and Marcia in the front row. She knew that when they saw her sitting with their nemesis Houdini, they would realize she had visited them as a spy.

As Houdini calmly started his testimony, he urged the committee to vote for the bill. He said that the fortune tellers, clairvoyants, astrologers, and fake mediums were out to cheat their customers. No one was able to predict the future, and there was no evidence that ghosts sent messages through mediums.

"Millions of dollars are stolen by clairvoyants and mediums in America every year, and I can prove it," he told the committee. "A fraudulent medium is in the dirtiest profession in the world."

A committee member inquired whether Houdini believed in astrology.

"I do not believe in astrology," answered Houdini. "They can not tell from a chunk of mud millions of miles away what is going to happen to me."

Houdini asked Rose Mackenberg to tell the congressmen what had happened during her investigations. Under oath, she testified about paying for sittings with ten Washington mediums. None of them was legitimate, she said.

When she visited Jane Coates, Mackenberg reported, the medium claimed to see a blue haze around her. According to Coates, the spirits predicted that Mackenberg would soon die unless she got over being nervous.

And there was more. Coates said that she sensed a strangled man who she believed was Mackenberg's dead husband. She also saw Mackenberg's two children who had died. One was her daughter, Lena.

Mackenberg informed the committee that she'd never been married or had children.

Glaring, Coates made a move toward Mackenberg, loudly and vehemently denying all of it. A committee member told her to sit down.

Next Mackenberg recounted her visit to Madame Marcia, who charged her $10 (about $150 today). The astrologer claimed to smell cancer around Mackenberg. Then she bragged that several US senators came to her for readings. According to Marcia, said Mackenberg, "Almost all the people in the White House believed in spiritualism."

Houdini sits with Senator Arthur Capper of Kansas during the February 26, 1926, hearing for the fortune-telling bill. According to Rose Mackenberg's later testimony, Capper was one of the senators that the mediums said visited them regularly. Seated directly behind Houdini and Capper are several mediums. Jane Coates is visible between the two men.

Bringing up Jane Coates again, Mackenberg revealed that the medium had told her, "I know for a fact that there have been spiritual seances held at the White House with President Coolidge and his family." Not only that, Mackenberg continued, but she also said, "I have a number of Senators who visit me here." Coates then mentioned that Senators Capper, Watson, Dill, and Fletcher had come to her for readings.

Coates screamed that it was false, again interrupting Mackenberg's testimony. Marcia shouted her protest, too. Spectators cried "Liar!" at Houdini and Mackenberg.

Houdini joined the uproar, calling the mediums and clairvoyants "crooks and criminals."

This posed photograph demonstrates how mediums convinced sitters that they were receiving a message through a spirit trumpet. Houdini performed this trick at a May 1926 hearing before a House of Representatives committee.

Former medium Annie Benninghofen (right) shows Houdini how she created messages in the dark séance room by making a spirit trumpet appear to float near a sitter's ear. Because the medium gave no sign that she was speaking and holding the trumpet, the sitter didn't realize that she—not a ghost—was the source of the message. When this photo was taken in April 1926, Benninghofen had left the medium business after admitting to thirty years of deceptive practices.

Finally, the committee chair quieted the room, and Houdini continued his testimony with a demonstration of how mediums created spirit voices.

He held a séance trumpet next to the ear of one of the lawmakers. The congressman reported hearing a voice say, "Your plans are arranged for. How are you?"

Houdini did the same for a congresswoman who asked to receive her own message through the trumpet. She said that she heard her name: "Hello, Edith Rogers."

Both representatives were perplexed. No sound came from Houdini's lips. Even spectators within 2 feet (0.6 m) of him heard nothing.

The shouting from the irate audience broke out again, louder than before. When the committee failed to get the commotion under control, the members adjourned the hearing for two days.

The raucous argument between those in favor of and those against the bill spilled into the hallway. Houdini nearly got into a fistfight with a man who tried to punch him for his scathing insults of mediums. Bystanders pulled them apart.

Mackenberg hadn't anticipated just how much her testimony would "shock, frighten and enrage" people. But she had managed to remain calm under fire. One newspaper reporter described her as "quiet-mannered" and "soft-voiced."

## SCANDAL

The press recognized a scandalous story. Newspapers everywhere carried articles about the hearing and the alleged table tipping at the White House. When a reporter interviewed Coates, she angrily refuted Rose Mackenberg's testimony. She clarified that she didn't tell Mackenberg that séances were held *at* the White House; she said they were held "under the shadow of the White House."

WASHINGTON TIMES HOME EDITION

THE NATIONAL DAILY

NO. 13,557   Entered as second-class matter at Postoffice at Washington, D. C.   WASHINGTON, TUESDAY, MAY 18, 1926   Published Daily   THREE CENTS

SPIRIT SEANCES AT WHITE HOUSE

Newspapers eagerly reported on the dramatic scenes involving Houdini, Mackenberg, and several Washington mediums. This is from the *Washington Times*, May 18, 1926.

(left to right) President Warren Harding (1865–1923), Florence Harding, Grace Coolidge, and future president Calvin Coolidge (1872–1933). This photograph was taken in March 1921 when Harding and Coolidge (with their wives) arrived in Washington for their inauguration. After Harding died in August 1923, Vice President Coolidge became president, serving until 1929.

Astrologer Madame Marcia claimed Florence Harding had been a regular customer. Medium Jane Coates told Rose Mackenberg that the Coolidges held séances in the White House.

The news forced the White House to issue a quick denial, stating that séances had never taken place there while the Coolidges were residents. Belief in the supernatural was considered a political liability, in part because of the long public campaign against fraudulent mediums by Houdini and others. And for decades, mainstream religions had been vocal in criticizing spiritualism.

The next day, Houdini dropped off a letter at the White House for the president. In it, he said he was sorry Coolidge's name had been brought into the controversy. He personally didn't believe that séances went on in the White House. His investigator had only reported what she'd been told by a medium. Along with the letter was Mackenberg's signed statement repeating what she'd testified in the hearing.

Houdini wasn't the only one to doubt the Calvin Coolidge story. A *New York Times* editorial published later that week said, "The President's cool New England mind is about the very last to have any patience with things of that sort. Moreover, the evidence presented is worse than worthless."

On Thursday, May 20, the hearings resumed. This time about 300 people crowded into the hearing room to watch.

Houdini knew how to make a dramatic gesture that the press would notice. He tossed $10,000 in cash on the committee table. He repeated his challenge to give it to a medium who could, then and there, exhibit supernatural power that he could not replicate.

Madame Marcia (Grace Champney Marcia) in 1921. The astrologer claimed to have predicted President Warren Harding's 1920 election and 1923 death.

Madame Marcia cried, "That money belongs to me."

She said that she deserved it for predicting President Harding's election and death. But since she didn't announce her prediction until after the events occurred, she didn't qualify for Houdini's reward.

When none of the other mediums in the room came forward, Houdini packed up the money and offered to demonstrate a séance manifestation of his own. He performed a baffling spirit slate trick containing a message from Benjamin Franklin.

Jane Coates called out, "He is demonstrating that he is a spiritualist."

Houdini explained to the committee how he had done the trick using a magic trick, deduction, and a few guesses. He wasn't a spiritualist, and he didn't employ any supernatural aids.

When Coates had her chance to testify to the committee, she accused Houdini of using black magic to hypnotize Rose Mackenberg. She again denied telling Mackenberg that the Coolidges engaged in table tipping.

"In my mind," she said, "I was thinking of Mrs. Harding, who openly visited mediums and many connected with her during Mr. Harding's administration [did, too]."

The hearings continued another day, and more accusations and denials flew back and forth. Mackenberg told how dozens of spiritualists and mediums tried to recruit her for their church and sold her certificates of ordination. Coates, Marcia, and other opponents of the bill repeatedly interrupted her as she reported about her Washington investigations.

## Certificate of Ordination

This is to Certify, THAT *Mrs. Annie W. Benninghofen* was, on the *14th* day of *February*, 1912, at the *First Spiritualists* (HERE PUT NAME OF SOCIETY) *Temple Society* (OR CHURCH) in the City of *Hamilton* County of *Butler* and State of *Ohio*, regularly ordained as a Minister of the Gospel of Spiritualism by the *State* Association *of Ohio*, in accordance with the Laws and Services of Ordination of the **National Spiritualists' Association of the United States of America**, a religious body, incorporated in the District of Columbia, of which body, said *State* Association *of Ohio* is a subordinate State Organization;

And that the said *Ohio State Association* is authorized to perform all the Rites and Ceremonies, including Marriage, pertaining to the Religion of Spiritualism, and that h *er* acts as such Minister are entitled to full Faith and Credit; subject, however, to the laws of the various states governing the performance of the marriage ceremony.

AS WITNESS the seal of the said *State* Association *of Ohio*, a body corporate, and the signature of the President thereof, attested by the Secretary, this *14th* day of *February*, in the year nineteen hundred and *twelve*

24
15  11    august
        a
200
J. E. D. Shirly

*D. A. Herrick* **President**
*Carl A. Sollinger* **Secretary**

40966

Houdini's niece and investigator, Julia Sawyer, testified about her visits to fake mediums. Other witnesses described how they had been cheated of their money by fortune tellers and mediums.

Mediums and supporters of spiritualism defended their work, insisting it was respectable in every way. Several discussed the importance of the religion in their lives. This bill, they said, persecuted spiritualists. One argued that the police were already able to handle scams by dishonest mediums and fortune tellers. There was no need for laws against everyone else.

At one point, a spiritualist witness made disparaging remarks about the religious views of Houdini and Representative Sol Bloom, the bill's author. Both men were Jewish. Houdini shot

Rose Mackenberg told the congressional committee that bogus ordination as a spiritualist minister was a way for mediums to claim they practiced a religion, protecting them from fraud laws. She testified that she had paid for several such certificates herself. This one made Annie Benninghofen a minister of the Gospel of Spiritualists. Benninghofen later confessed to being a fake medium.

back, "My religion and my belief in the Almighty has been assailed . . . I have always believed and I will always believe."

Houdini's dramatic appearance and Mackenberg's bombshell statements about the president and senators generated national attention. In the end, though, the bill didn't get enough support to pass. Some in Congress thought the matter was too trivial to require regulation. Others accepted the argument that the law would trample the First Amendment rights of a religious group.

Not only did the spiritualists win their fight, but mediums and fortune tellers also found that the press coverage brought them more business. And although Houdini maintained that he had not gone before Congress as a publicity stunt, his four days of testimony again put his name in headlines across the country.

Houdini's poster advertises his 1926 stage show that combines magic tricks and illusions, his escapes, and an exposure of fake mediums.

## INJURIES

After a summer break, Houdini took his three-act show back on the road in September 1926. The debunking of fraudulent mediums still made up the third act. Houdini told a reporter that his crusade against deceptive mediums had "reduced materially the number of these vultures by exposing them and their methods." That knowledge motivated him to keep on with his work.

On October 11, he was performing in Albany, New York. During the Water Torture Cell, Houdini felt a sharp pain in his leg before he was dunked headfirst into the tank of water. Something had gone wrong on the cover where his feet were clamped onto the equipment.

After his feet were released, a doctor sitting in the audience came up to examine him. He told Houdini that the ankle seemed to be broken. The magician should go to the hospital for X-rays.

Houdini continued with the show, but he followed the advice after the final curtain. Doctors at the hospital confirmed that he had a break in his left ankle. They immobilized the ankle with a splint and recommended that he stay off the foot so that the bone could heal. Houdini wasn't going to do that. He fashioned his own brace which allowed him to perform, although he couldn't completely hide his limp. He would never use the Water Torture Cell again.

By the next week, the troupe had traveled by train to Montreal, Canada. Rose Mackenberg and Julia Sawyer had been attending séances in the city and taking notes about the mediums. Once again, Houdini used their research in the third act of his show.

Besides his theater performances, Houdini accepted the invitation of McGill University's psychology department to speak to students about magic, spiritual frauds, and his escapes. Two days after that lecture, in late morning on October 22, three McGill students visited the theater. He had invited one of them to sketch his portrait.

Houdini stretched out on a couch in his dressing room, propping himself up with pillows and reading his mail while the young man drew. One of the other students asked Houdini questions about his work and his interests. Was it true the escape artist could withstand a hard blow to his gut?

Houdini responded that his back and arm muscles were exceptionally strong, and he invited the three students to feel them. The student asked again about the abdominal muscles. He wondered if it would be all right to punch Houdini there.

Houdini agreed. But before he had a chance to stand up and brace himself, the young man struck him several times.

Caught off guard, Houdini winced before telling the student to stop. The artist quickly finished his drawing and showed Houdini the portrait. Then the three students left the dressing room.

Later that Friday afternoon, Houdini had pain in his abdomen. He thought the muscles might have cramped up or been injured by the punch. He went on stage for his evening show, though it was a struggle. In the middle of the night, Houdini developed terrible cramps.

Throughout his career, he had experienced many injuries. Neither a sore abdomen nor a broken ankle was going to stop him from performing. Forcing himself to keep on, he made his final Montreal appearance the following evening. Then he and the troupe boarded the train to their next stop in Detroit, Michigan.

By the time they arrived, Houdini was running a high fever. He had severe chills, and the pain was much worse. His team arranged for a doctor to meet them at the theater and check out the magician. According to a statement the doctor made later, he told Houdini that his appendix might be the problem and advised him to go to the hospital.

Houdini chose to wait. The theater was standing room only, and he had a show to present to his audience. But though he tried, he wasn't able to perform all of his tricks and illusions in the two-and-a-half-hour program. At the end, he had to be helped off the stage.

When Houdini returned to his hotel, Bess insisted that he get medical help immediately. That night, two more doctors came to his room and examined him. His temperature was 104 degrees and his pain had increased—both signs of infection. They agreed he required hospitalization right away. In the early hours of Monday, October 25, Houdini finally allowed himself to be admitted to Detroit's Grace Hospital.

Several hours later, surgeons operated on the magician. They discovered that his appendix had ruptured, spreading bacteria throughout his abdominal cavity. Surgeons removed the damaged appendix, yet they didn't have antibiotics in those days to fight the resulting massive infection. Doctors were pessimistic about Houdini's chances.

Two of his brothers and his sister traveled from New York to be with him in Detroit, joining Bess and Houdini's team. They all waited anxiously.

Although he seemed to rally midweek, Houdini needed another surgery on Friday. The lining of his abdomen was inflamed as a result of the infection, a condition called peritonitis.

The operation didn't help. By the early hours of Sunday, Houdini was slipping away, and he knew it. He said to his brother, who sat next to his hospital bed, "I'm tired of fighting, Dash. I guess this thing is going to get me."

Those would be Harry Houdini's last words. On Sunday, October 31, at 1:26 in the afternoon, he died at age fifty-two. It was Halloween.

# Death Ends Career Of Magician Houdini

# Houdini Dead And Secrets of Magic With Him

# HOUDINI, MAGICIAN, IS NO MORE; DIES AFTER OPERATION

## COLLAPSED EIGHT DAYS AGO AT THE END OF OPENING PERFORMANCE

Houdini's hospitalization and death were front-page news around the country. These headlines appeared on November 1, 1926, the day after his Halloween death, in the *Kennebec Journal* [Augusta, ME] (top), *San Angelo* [TX] *Evening Standard* (bottom left), and *Seward* [AK] *Daily Gateway* (bottom right).

## WAITING FOR A MESSAGE

Houdini's death certificate attributed his demise to peritonitis caused by a ruptured appendix. An investigation by Houdini's life insurance company concluded that the blow to his abdomen had accidentally caused the damage.

His body was taken by train back to New York City, where 2,000 mourners attended his funeral. Harry Houdini was buried next to his parents in Machpelah Cemetery in Queens.

His passing brought tributes from the many people who admired his abilities and accomplishments. But not everyone mourned his death. One spiritualist leader from Rochester, New York—where the Fox sisters got their start—was quick to voice his opinion about the man who had long campaigned against mediums. He told a reporter that he had warned Houdini that "old Father Time and the undertaker would convince him" of the truth of spiritualism.

Houdini had promised Bess, as well as several friends, that he would communicate with them after death if he could. He gave each person a different secret code that would prove the message was truly from him, not made up by a fraudulent medium.

No messages came.

Newspapers frequently reported on mediums who held séances to contact Houdini's spirit. In January 1927, Bess offered $10,000 to any medium who brought her word from Harry. She received dozens of letters from mediums who claimed they had heard from him. None even slightly resembled the message she and Harry had agreed upon.

Arthur Conan Doyle wrote Bess a letter saying that he felt sure Houdini had psychic powers. He assured her in late January 1927, "There is, after death, a period of complete rest which varies in different cases. When H. has emerged from this, I am quite sure, knowing his determined character, that he will get back to you."

Houdini's wife, Bess, and his brother Theodore, nicknamed "Dash," at his grave in New York City

He sent Bess names of mediums who could help her contact her husband. Later he passed on messages from two mediums that he believed were signs from Houdini. Bess could tell they were fake.

Conan Doyle wasn't the only spiritualist who thought Houdini had special abilities. "Almost all medium and spiritual workers in the country are of the belief that he was a medium," explained an American spiritualist leader. They were certain that was how he made his escapes.

Another spiritualist said that Houdini had great intuitive powers. "I hope now that he realizes the truth of spiritualism."

One spiritualist's claim made headlines in January 1929. He revealed that during a séance at Bess Houdini's home, her dead husband sent a message using their secret code. The decrypted word was "Believe."

But it turned out to be a hoax. The code had been published the year before in a biography of Houdini. Bess had cooperated with the author in writing the book.

This photograph was taken at the final séance Bess Houdini held to contact her husband's spirit, on October 31, 1936, the tenth anniversary of his death.

After many years of waiting in vain for a message, Bess gave spirit communication one more chance on October 31, 1936, the tenth anniversary of Houdini's death. "Houdini could escape anything alive," she told a reporter before the public séance. "If he cannot escape from the 'other side' in 10 years, then I cannot believe that anyone can."

Her well-publicized séance was held on the roof of the Knickerbocker Hotel in Hollywood, California. As many as 300 guests attended, including several scientists, reporters, and friends. The event was broadcast on the radio.

Bess and her closest friends sat at a long table draped in red. Lying in front of them was a spirit trumpet, spirit slates, paper and pencil, a silver bell, and pair of locked handcuffs. Everything was ready to receive a message from Harry Houdini.

"Houdini, are you here?" cried out Bess's business manager. "We have waited, Houdini, oh so long." He begged Houdini to give a sign by speaking through the trumpet or ringing the bell or lifting the table. "Come through, Harry!"

Bess called to him, too.

Everyone waited. Nothing happened. There was no sign, only silence.

"Houdini did not come through," Bess said at last. "I do not believe that Houdini can come back to me or to anyone. . . . I do not believe that ghosts or spirits exist." She turned off a small red lamp by Houdini's portrait. "It is finished. Good night, Harry."

A full-page tribute to Houdini published in *Genii* magazine more than ten years after his death. His April 6 birthdate perpetuates the myth that Houdini created. He was really born on March 24.

## CHAPTER NINE

# THE WOMAN WITH A THOUSAND HUSBANDS

*"All they ever can say is that they are well and happy."*
*—Rose Mackenberg, 1937*

Rose Mackenberg had attended about three hundred séances while working with Harry Houdini, and not a single one produced an authentic message from the afterlife. She no longer believed in ghosts and the supernatural as she once had.

Mackenberg understood why grieving people clung to the idea that they could communicate with a loved one. But this was what made them targets of unscrupulous mediums. Her experience as a detective and spirit debunker gave her the skills she needed to stop these spook crooks.

"My secret service under the direction of Harry Houdini . . . taught me many things," she said. "Self-control, courage, resourcefulness and the ability not to let myself be thrown off a scent by astonishment."

## RICH RELATIONS

In the late 1920s, Mackenberg established a business as an expert on mediums and their scams. Building on her association with Houdini, she called herself "Houdini's Chief Investigator and Private Detective."

Law firms hired her to investigate cases in which a client lost money or changed a will after visiting a medium. Banks, insurance companies, and detective agencies came to her for help in gathering evidence when their customers were cheated by mediums and fortune tellers.

Mackenberg worked with law enforcement, too. In one case, the authorities received complaints about a medium who convinced his sitters to invest in phony businesses. He took their cash, but the victims couldn't prove they'd been cheated. The police asked Mackenberg to trap the swindler.

She visited the medium dressed as a wealthy widow, telling him that she didn't know what her husband wanted her to do with her inheritance of several thousand dollars. During the séance, her dead spouse's spirit told her—through the medium—that she should invest in a certain company. The medium offered to arrange the transaction for her.

Mackenberg said that she didn't have enough cash with her, but she could leave a check as a small deposit. She would come back the next day with the rest of the money in cash.

The medium agreed to this arrangement. Mackenberg acted helpless, fretting that she had trouble writing. Could he fill out the check for her?

Once he had done that and given her a receipt for her money, Mackenberg had the evidence the police needed. His handwriting connected the medium to the bogus company. When she returned to pay the rest of the money, she took along a police officer carrying an arrest warrant. The medium was convicted and sent to jail.

Mackenberg frequently pretended to be a vulnerable widow. No matter which of Mackenberg's imaginary husbands spoke to her at séances, they always told her they were happy and well in the afterlife.

At one séance, she asked her husband in spirit land if the novel she had just finished writing would sell well. His "ghost"

Dressed in one of her disguises, Rose Mackenberg poses as a gullible widow with some savings.

responded through a spirit trumpet: Oh yes, the book was going to be a huge success, though she needed to adjust the final chapter.

Mackenberg had trapped another medium in a lie. There was no final chapter because there was no book—or dead husband.

One of her favorite ghost husbands was Walter. "I've received so many messages from Walter," she said, "that I'm getting really fond of him." The only problem was that "he's always telling me to give part of his insurance money to the medium."

Mackenberg picked her disguise, depending on the situation. She went to one séance dressed as a young woman. Using her alias Frances Raud, she told the medium that her Aunt Sarah (a made-up person) had died and left her the entire estate. It was quite a bit of money, and Frances didn't know what her aunt wanted her to do with the inheritance. Could the medium contact Aunt Sarah?

Closing her eyes, the medium seemed to fall into a trance. She groaned and muttered in an eerie voice, "I am watching over you, darling."

Frances asked how she should use the inherited money.

"Spend it any way you like, darling," replied Aunt Sarah's spirit, "except that I want you to give $500 to the medium for her church."

As the voice faded away, the medium opened her eyes. She acted as though she had no memory of what had just happened.

When Frances filled her in, the medium quickly handed her a blank check, saying that Frances could make it out for the $500 then and there.

Mackenberg had caught another spook crook in the act.

Surprisingly, none of the medium's spirit connections informed her of Mackenberg's true identity. In fact, no medium *ever* figured out who she was until after her investigation ended and the fraudster was exposed.

## BEWARE THE SCAMMERS!

Time and time again, Mackenberg witnessed gullible sitters who never doubted that they heard a ghost's voice through a spirit trumpet, no matter how obvious the trick was. At one séance, the medium had laryngitis. Every spirit that talked through the trumpet had laryngitis, too.

When Mackenberg pretended to be a wealthy widow, mediums never failed to call up her dead husband's spirit.

In this disguise from the late 1930s, Mackenberg gave the impression of a naïve young woman who could be easily fooled.

In 1949, Rose Mackenberg demonstrates a trick used by mediums at séances. She stated several times over the years that she was one of the people with whom Houdini had made a pact to send a message after his death. "I have never as yet received the slightest semblance of a bona fide message along the lines upon which we had agreed," she said.

Mackenberg dedicated herself to protecting people from these ghost scams. "I'm just trying to expose the charlatans who prey upon the public by claiming they can speak to the dead," she said. "So can I but they don't answer."

She soon found a way to reach more people—the press. By recounting her experiences in newspaper and magazine articles, she educated readers about the techniques the psychic con artists used.

In one article, Mackenberg told how she caught a dishonest medium because he smelled. When the man greeted her before the séance, she detected the strong, unpleasant odor of his shaving lotion. During the séance, two spirits appeared dressed in different costumes. Both ghosts reeked of the same scent.

Mackenberg later returned for a second séance. This time she took along an assistant armed with a hidden flash camera. When the spirit of an American Indian passed near her in the dimly lit room, Mackenberg seized his ankle. Her assistant snapped the photograph. The ghostly figure was the foul-smelling medium in costume. Another crook exposed!

She explained to readers how mediums used alcohol to see questions sealed in an envelope, a trick which persuaded countless people of a medium's psychic ability. One reason séance rooms often had an unusual fragrance was to mask the alcohol odor. She once quipped, "I smell a rat before I smell the incense."

Mackenberg warned about blackmail danger. Many who sought out a medium had personal troubles. The medium could expertly pull out information about those problems until clients had divulged much more than they intended. Armed with these secrets, the medium threatened to tell all unless paid for silence.

Mackenberg was careful to state that she respected spiritualism as a religion and thought everyone had the freedom to worship as they wished. Still, she admitted that she didn't believe in what the religion promised. It seemed unlikely to her that "former husbands marching across a dark room or shouting through a $3.45 trumpet are the means by which a more spiritual world would be revealed to us."

## GOING TO COURT

In September 1934, Rose Mackenberg accompanied a Philadelphia newspaper reporter on a visit to Camp Silver Belle, in Ephrata, Pennsylvania. The camp was run by well-known spiritualist Ethel Post and her husband, and mediums gathered there each summer. Silver Belle was the name of Ethel Post's spirit guide.

Using the skills Mackenberg learned from Houdini, she helped the reporter with his exposé of Camp Silver Belle. His article disclosed how phony mediums used trumpet séances and message writing to deceive those who hoped for signs from loved ones. The spiritual healers charged customers for bogus cures.

Attending a séance held by Ethel Post, Mackenberg and the reporter asked to hear from the spirits of several specific people. Post produced messages from all of them, even though two were still alive and the rest never existed.

In another session, Post had each audience member write a question for a spirit on a card. After signing the card, the person handed it in. Post assured the group that she'd use her powers to give the spirits' answers.

She prepared for the reading by having an assistant place two small discs over her eyes and tie a black silk handkerchief around her head. Post said this double cover would shut out the light so that she could concentrate better.

Now securely blindfolded, Post reached for each card. She appeared to be intensely focusing and pondering over the

Because mediums often tried to take advantage of older women, Mackenberg used this disguise in many of her medium visits. She posed for the photograph in 1945.

question. At times, she touched her finger against the silk blindfold, gathering her psychic energy. Then she announced the message and gave an answer. The audience was astounded that she knew who had asked each question. They were thrilled by her answers.

How did Ethel Post do it? Mackenberg had seen the trick before. The discs on Post's eyes actually made it easier for her to read the cards. When the silk blindfold was placed over her face, it pushed the top of each disc against the bone above her eyebrows. That allowed a gap beneath the disc's bottom. By tilting her head, the medium could see from under the discs and the blindfold.

In his newspaper article about the visit to Camp Silver Belle, the reporter called the spiritualist retreat "a three-ring circus of flim-flam."

After the article was published, spiritualists went on the attack. *Psychic News*, a British spiritualist newspaper, ran a story about Rose Mackenberg. It reported that she sent out proposals to American newspapers offering to help them expose mediums in their city. Her letter, the paper said, made the selling point that these feature articles would boost the newspaper's circulation.

*Psychic News* told its readers that Rose Mackenberg "has for many years made a living preying upon a religion against which she has been and continues to be prejudiced." In an act of intimidation, the newspaper published her New York City home address for all her enemies to see.

That wasn't the end of the Camp Silver Belle story. Two months after the exposé appeared, seventy-year-old widow Mary Stephan died. A wealthy supporter of Camp Silver Belle and the Posts, she left thousands of dollars to the spiritualist retreat in her will. Stephan had no children, but a dozen members of her extended family challenged the will in court. They argued that Mary had been duped by the spiritualists.

The family's attorney arranged for testimony from Rose Mackenberg and the reporter who had written the exposé. They both said that Mary Stephan and her husband had been misled about the spirit manifestations and messages at Camp Silver Belle. In court, Mackenberg demonstrated how the mediums there used sleight of hand and other tricks to deceive sitters.

In the end, the judge ruled that Mary Stephan's will could not grant the money to the spiritualists due to a technical legal issue. Camp Silver Belle lost the case, and the court granted Mary Stephan's heirs the money instead.

The spiritualist press continued to comment on Mackenberg's ghost-busting articles and lectures. Making fun of her disguises, one columnist said, "She would make a better living as a scarecrow than as a pseudo psychic investigator."

## MEDIUM TOURS

By the summer of 1945, World War II was drawing to a close after four years of US involvement. More than 400,000 Americans had died fighting the war, and the public's attraction to spiritualism had increased again. Mackenberg visited neighborhoods where nearly every house had a medium's sign outside.

Mourners at a Kentucky gravesite around 1940. When a person died, the survivors felt intense grief, making them susceptible to fraudsters who promised to contact the deceased—for a fee. Mackenberg saw a dramatic uptick in American mediums during World War II (1941–45) as the number of war casualties skyrocketed. "The anguish of friends and relatives of dead, wounded or missing servicemen," she said, "offers a fertile field for heartless deception."

That summer, Mackenberg took several reporters on a tour of mediums in their cities. Afterward, each journalist wrote a series of articles about the experience.

Mackenberg and the reporters always had to pay for a séance. Although it was illegal in many cities for a medium or fortune teller to charge a fee, the police usually didn't do anything about it unless someone complained. When mediums asked for donations before a séance, they said that spirits would be insulted if someone gave too little. For those who were desperate to receive a message, this was coercion to shell out cash even if the person couldn't afford it.

When she visited mediums, Mackenberg sometimes took along a reporter who later wrote a newspaper article about the frauds. Here she prepares her outfit for a 1945 tour of Philadelphia with a reporter from the *Philadelphia Evening Bulletin*. His article exposed how séance scams swindled servicemen's families. To create her sitter's identity, she carefully chose her dress, hat, jewelry, fingernail polish, and makeup.

In Detroit, Michigan, Mackenberg and a male reporter visited numerous mediums, using made-up names and pretending to be a dating couple. They asked about fictional friends and relatives who had passed away, including Mackenberg's (nonexistent) dead husband and the reporter's (still alive) mother. The medium provided an update on each in the afterlife.

Communicating through a spirit trumpet, Mackenberg's husband Bill thanked her for his funeral and said he approved of her marriage to the reporter. She asked about their friend Howard, who had been killed when his ship sunk in the Pacific Ocean. Bill relayed the message through the trumpet that he guided Howard to the spirit world.

Nobody named Bill or Howard existed in Mackenberg's life.

At a séance with another medium, the reporter wanted to know if a story he'd written would sell to a particular publisher. Definitely, replied the medium.

The reporter had never written the story, and he'd invented the publisher's name.

A woman sitter at the séance sought a message about her three sons who were still overseas with the military. The trumpet voice said that one of them would not return healthy from the war. The woman sobbed.

Mackenberg considered such mediums "mean and contemptible." A mother put her trust in mediums and fortune

122

tellers to reveal her son's fate when she was worried about his well-being or was mourning his death. Would he recover from his wounds? Would the missing soldier be found? Had the dead man safely passed into the hereafter? Mackenberg thought it was cruel that fraudsters made up stories and falsely raised or dashed hopes.

Wartime scams by mediums targeted grieving mothers and widows. The spirit message from the mourner's dead loved one would tell her to donate to a spiritualist church part of the insurance money she received upon his death. The medium, of course, promised to pass on the money to the church.

In Chicago, Illinois, Mackenberg and a reporter visited several mediums. At one séance, Mackenberg dressed up as an older woman with a hearing aid. She asked about her nephew Bill. The medium said that Bill didn't suffer, but she saw an amputated leg. Every time the medium gave a message, Mackenberg reacted as if it could be accurate. That kept the medium elaborating with more details from spirits of people who never existed.

Another Chicago medium gave messages to a small audience. She said she felt a young man's spirit in the room. Mackenberg asked if it was Harold, her son who had been killed in an explosion. The medium immediately reported that Harold was standing beside Mackenberg, and he looked just like her.

Mackenberg had never had a son.

No matter where Mackenberg and the reporters went that summer, mediums provided messages from imaginary individuals. But the investigators weren't able to check out as many séances as they'd hoped. Some mediums were so busy with people concerned about sons, husbands, and friends who had died in the war that they had no open appointments for two months.

## THE GHOST DETECTIVE

Besides her articles in magazines and newspapers, Mackenberg presented hundreds of lectures and entertaining programs for women's clubs, community groups, colleges, and private parties. She called one of her talks "Phantoms and Fakes." Another was "Debunking the Ghost Racket."

She often used Houdini's approach of holding a séance on

Mackenberg performed demonstrations of medium tricks for live audiences and on television. In this 1951 photograph, she shows how a medium working with an assistant can make a trumpet hang in the air and produce a spirit voice. By cupping her hand, Mackenberg creates the eerie voice. In an actual séance, this would go on in the dark. The assistant who holds the trumpet is dressed completely in black. Mackenberg wears long black gloves so that sitters can't see what her hands are doing.

stage and then showing how the tricks were done. During her presentation, Mackenberg explained how a medium collected enough information about a sitter to make the séance seem mystical. She demonstrated dozens of the methods employed by fraudulent mediums to fool their customers, including the spirit trumpet, the floating table, spirit slates, ectoplasm, and the flying ghosts.

At the end of her talks, Mackenberg frequently remarked, "My ghosts have been treated by luminous paint. They may look like spirits, but believe me they ain't."

Despite her warnings, she encountered audience members who declared that the medium they regularly visited was genuine and never used such tricks. Mackenberg asked the person to share a miracle the favorite medium performed. Then she replicated it. Her demonstration opened the eyes of some people. But Mackenberg knew that others would never change their mind no matter what proof of deceit she provided.

Rose Mackenberg reached more of the public when she was interviewed on nationally broadcast radio programs in the 1930s and 1940s. Listeners heard her describe how she trapped fake mediums. When television took hold in the 1950s, she made guest appearances on several shows. Interviewers sometimes called her "a female Sherlock Holmes."

For more than thirty years, Mackenberg earned her living as a

Mackenberg tilts a table in this séance trick. A wooden rod extends from the glove on her right hand and hooks under the table edge. This gives her enough leverage to make the table move. A sitter wouldn't be able to spot the rod, especially in a dimly lit room.

ghost detective. She'd seen interest in the supernatural remain high. In one estimate from 1953, 200,000 mediums practiced in towns and cities around the country. Americans spent millions of dollars to visit them.

Mackenberg concluded that some mediums might truly believe they had special ability to see the future or communicate with the dead. But nothing she'd witnessed ever convinced her that these powers were real. She feared that the ghost racket wouldn't stop until wars ended and people had no more problems.

After a lifetime as a New York City resident, Rose Mackenberg died of circulation and heart disease in 1968 at the age of seventy-five. Unfortunately, the illness affected her brain during the last months of her life.

She never married or became a mother. Yet Mackenberg reported receiving messages from "1500 husbands, 3000 children, innumerable grandchildren, and enough mothers, fathers, grandmothers, grandfathers, sisters, brothers, cousins, aunts and uncles to populate a fair-sized town." She even got barked messages from her imaginary dog, Spunky. Despite investigating more than a thousand mediums, the spirit sleuth found only frauds.

"It's really awful disappointing," she once told a reporter. "I'd love to find one good solid ghost I could sit down and have a pleasant chat with."

She never did.

# MARY SULLIVAN

In 1931, the New York City Police Department ran a campaign against fortune tellers, mediums, clairvoyants, astrologers, and others who were swindling New Yorkers. These scammers cheated customers out of about $25 million a year (about $450 million today).

The police department wasn't even sure how many fraudsters were operating in the city but guessed there were about 20,000. New players constantly came on the scene. While most mediums avoided trouble by saying they were practicing the spiritualist religion, fortune tellers and astrologers who charged a fee were violating the city's law. The penalty was up to six months in jail.

Because almost all the customers and fortune tellers were women, the campaign used disguised female police officers to catch the crooks. At one point, 100 policewomen were involved. The head of the bureau of policewomen, Mary Sullivan, was put in charge of the campaign.

Mary Sullivan (about 1878–1950) in 1911 when she first joined the New York Police Department

## GOING UNDERCOVER

Sullivan was the daughter of Irish immigrants and grew up in Manhattan. Coming from a family connected to the NYPD for two generations, she joined the department in 1911 when she was in her early thirties.

At first, Sullivan served as a matron who guarded women prisoners. She advanced to detective and worked undercover to catch criminals, including murderers. In 1926, she became director of policewomen, eventually taking charge of 165 female officers.

Even before the 1931 campaign, Sullivan had had many years of experience arresting fortune tellers and mediums. Like Rose Mackenberg, she visited in disguise, making up a story about her problems. When the fortune teller collected her money, the policewoman paid in marked bills. Minutes later, another officer entered the room, and they arrested the crook.

Sullivan had a special reason for wanting to track down fortune tellers. When she was eight, her five-year-old brother wandered from the house and never returned. Sullivan's mother visited fortune tellers for years, hoping to learn his fate. They told her numerous stories, which were all lies. "The repeated disappointments my mother suffered," Sullivan said, "caused her as much pain as if the boy had been lost to her many times instead of only once."

## FORTUNE TELLER CONS

Sullivan was aware that some people went to fortune tellers because they needed hope or were afraid to make decisions on their own. Fortune tellers offered others the promise of personal prosperity and happiness. But sadly, Sullivan had seen too many New Yorkers make disastrous mistakes, lose their savings, or give up a good job based on what a fortune teller or medium said.

In one police case, a woman visited a neighborhood fortune teller and paid $10 (about $200 today). The fortune teller put the money into a black bag and sent it home with the woman.

When she opened it, there was $11 inside. The next time she visited the fortune teller, the woman handed over $40 (about $800 today) to put in the bag. At home, she found $46.

The superstitious woman was sure that mystical forces were involved, and she gave the fortune teller her savings of more than $4,000 (nearly $80,000 today) to put in the bag. When the woman returned home and opened the bag, there was only $20. By then, the fortune teller had disappeared.

In another swindle, a fortune teller told a customer that her bad luck was due to curses placed upon her. The fortune teller claimed she could lift the curse with a special medicine that cost a few hundred dollars.

For the NYPD's 1931 anti-fortune-telling campaign, Mary Sullivan worked with members of the Society of American Magicians (SAM) who helped in identifying and exposing the culprits. Like former SAM president Harry Houdini, these magicians knew how the deceptions were done and they wanted them stopped.

In addition to raids and arrests, the campaign included an education program to warn the public about the hoaxes. Newspaper articles reported on police cases, and magicians performed demonstrations of the tricks used on unsuspecting victims.

The effort to prevent illegal fortune-telling was a challenge. Sullivan wrote in 1938 that, though they'd done a fairly good job, "we've no hope of actually stamping out fortunetelling until that distant day when all human beings acquire common sense."

Sullivan retired in April 1946 after nearly thirty-five years with the police department. She died in 1950 at age seventy-one.

CHAPTER TEN

# THE SUPERNATURAL RACKET

"When the spirits come in at the door, common sense flies
out the window."
—*Rose Mackenberg, 1945*

When Harry Houdini was sixteen, he caught a medium cheating during a séance. The man reacted to the exposure by saying, "You've got to admit that I do more good than harm by consoling sorrowing people who long for a message from their loved ones!" Nearly 135 years later, many modern mediums defend their work the same way.

Houdini came to realize that this justification was false. For years, he collected tragic tales of disappointed and cheated victims of mediums' deceptions. The parade of victims has continued into the twenty-first century.

## PSYCHIC FRAUDS

Today's mediums are often called psychics, but the idea is the same. They claim to have supernatural abilities, such as receiving messages from the spirits or seeing the future.

Houdini never found a genuine medium who could communicate with the spirits. But he became friendly with several who admitted using tricks. In 1924, he visited the well-known medium, Anna Eva Fay (1851–1927), and they posed by the gazing ball in her garden near Boston.

By the time she was in her teens, Fay was performing séances. In the 1870s, she became famous as a stage medium, employing escapes the way the Davenport brothers had. Later she did a mind-reading act. During Houdini's visit, the retired Fay told him that she never believed in spiritualism and that she had used tricks to fool everyone.

Faked videos and photographs are used to convince people that ghosts and haunted houses are real. This "spirit" posed for a talented photographer who created the eerie image in 2019.

In 2022, people in the United States spent more than $2.2 billion a year on psychic services. Those businesses include mediums, clairvoyants, fortune tellers, astrologers, tarot card readers, palm readers, dream interpreters, and spiritual healers. One survey in 2009 showed that 30 million Americans had paid for advice from psychics.

When this much money is involved, swindlers are active. People from all walks of life, all income levels, and all ages have fallen prey to fraudulent psychics and mediums. One convicted crook was asked at her parole hearing whether there were any legitimate psychics. She replied, "If they are taking your money, they are not for real."

Vulnerable individuals are easy to trick. Perhaps a person has financial difficulties, is grief-stricken over a death, or feels crushing disappointment after a romantic breakup. The psychic listens to the client's troubles, is sympathetic, and gives advice. Soon the person becomes dependent on the psychic.

After fraudsters hook someone, they explain that the client has to keep paying or bad things will happen. One woman was told if she didn't continue sending money for protection from evil spirits, her children would die.

In the 1920s, Houdini lobbied lawmakers to ban fortune-telling and other psychic activities. Today the laws vary across the country. In some states, such as New York, it's illegal to pretend to use supernatural powers to answer questions, give advice, or fix a client's problems unless it's part of an entertainment show. Most mediums avoid the regulations by claiming to practice a religion.

Other states allow fortune-telling but require a license. To obtain one, a person has to pay a fee and might have to submit to a background check and fingerprinting. While a state may lack regulation against fortune-telling, cities within it can require a permit.

The websites of psychics, mediums, and fortune tellers usually contain a disclaimer in small print. It says that the service is for entertainment and for adults older than eighteen. Users of the service do so at their own risk. This disclaimer is designed to protect the psychic from being blamed if a customer acts on the psychic's words and later suffers financial, medical, or psychological harm.

Despite regulations, the police often don't follow up on law-breaking psychics unless someone complains. Clients of fraudulent psychics are frequently too embarrassed to go to the police once they realize they've been scammed.

Authorities have moved in, however, when a psychic extorts large amounts of money from customers. In many states, the crime is grand larceny if more than $1,000 has been stolen. This is a felony with serious penalties. Some twenty-first-century psychic fraud cases have involved millions.

## MISS CLEO

About twenty-five years ago, a woman known as Miss Cleo advertised on national television and in spam emails and telephone calls. Declaring that she was a psychic, Cleo offered a free tarot-card reading by phone. But none of it was free. People were unknowingly charged for their phone call and the reading.

Because Cleo had made deceptive claims in her advertising and billing, the Federal Trade Commission acted. This consumer protection agency fined Miss Cleo and the Psychic Readers Network, the company that employed her. The fine was $5 million, and the company had to return $500 million to customers who had been falsely charged a fee over a period of three years.

The scam went deeper than the financial fraud. When someone called the advertised phone number, a Psychic Readers employee pretended to give a reading. No matter who called, the "psychic" recited the caller's future from a pre-written script supplied by the company. Prosecutors stuck to the false advertising and fraud case because, they said, it was hard to prove in court that someone isn't a psychic.

## PSYCHIC ZOE

Ruth's life was spinning out of control. She was going through a messy divorce, and she was in physical pain from an accident. She felt hopeless. On a whim while she was on a business trip to New York City, she paid $5 for a reading by Psychic Zoe.

The psychic told Ruth that she suffered from a curse. Zoe could protect her and remove the curse so that Ruth felt content again. To do this, she advised Ruth to buy gold because of its power of protection. A gold coin guarded one person in Ruth's life. Psychic Zoe would put the gold in a special place where it steadily strengthened the protection. The psychic assured Ruth that if it didn't work, she could get her money back. Ruth handed over $18,000 for fifteen gold coins and a gold chain.

After Ruth returned to her home in Canada, Psychic Zoe constantly called and texted, saying that she'd seen tragedy ahead. To avoid this, Ruth needed additional gold protection. Ruth was afraid, so she kept paying Psychic Zoe.

This went on for more than three years. By then, Ruth had given Psychic Zoe $740,000 to erase the curses that were ruining her life. Although Ruth asked for her money, Zoe never reimbursed any of it as she'd promised. Nearly broke, Ruth finally realized she'd been cheated. She hired a private investigator who specialized in psychic scams.

Armed with the investigator's information, the New York City police found evidence that Psychic Zoe had stolen well over a million dollars from twenty of her customers. By 2018, the swindler was in jail for fraud and grand larceny. Because she pled guilty to her crimes, Psychic Zoe avoided a long prison sentence, though the judge ordered her to repay the victims. Ruth and the others received just a fraction of the money they had lost.

## THE FRAUDSTER FAMILY

Nine members of the Marks family ran several psychic businesses in Florida and New York City. They claimed to be clairvoyants and fortune tellers who communicated with the spirits and could help people with their troubles.

A woman, distraught about her failing marriage and her young son's accidental death, paid $12 million over several years for advice from one of the Marks family.

Another client bought $400,000 in gold coins to have his problems solved. When he later requested his money back, the psychic said she had buried it in a cemetery and couldn't remember where.

Before the nine were caught and arrested for fraud and money laundering in 2011, they had swindled tens of millions of

Fortune tellers often use tarot cards in their psychic readings.

dollars from their clients during a twenty-year period. Rose Marks, the family's matriarch and head of the business, was sentenced to ten years in federal prison.

### THE MISSING LOVER

In August 2013, Niall visited a New York City psychic. He sought help in reuniting with Michelle, whom he met at rehab in a different state. The psychic told Niall that she could contact the spirits, and she guaranteed to get rid of the evil ones that were keeping the lovers apart—for a fee. Niall was glad to pay anything to see Michelle again.

Then he found out from another source that Michelle had died. No problem, the psychic said. She could reincarnate Michelle—for a price. When the psychic identified a young woman as the new Michelle, Niall even tried to date her.

Over a period of twenty months, Niall paid the psychic more than $700,000 in cash and jewelry before he finally wised up and called the police. The psychic was arrested and charged with grand larceny.

## THE CROOKED CLAIRVOYANT

In Charlottesville, Virginia, Catherine ran a business offering various kinds of readings, including spirit, tarot card, palm, and astrological. She claimed that she was a medium who communicated with the spirits as well as a clairvoyant who could see the future and the past.

People came to her with their troubles, and Catherine promised to free them of the curses that plagued their life. All they had to do was give up valuables and cash which she would bury in a box. After the box was cleansed, she'd return their property. It could take time, but this process would get rid of the darkness. Sometimes Catherine told clients that they had to supply more money so that she could continue the cleansing.

Meanwhile, Catherine spent it all. She was arrested in 2016 for mail fraud and money laundering. She pled guilty and the court ordered her to pay more than $1 million to her victims, much less than she stole. Six of her customers had given her more than $2.3 million. Catherine was sentenced to serve thirty months in federal prison.

## THE PANDEMIC PSYCHIC

Rose Mackenberg noticed in the mid-1900s that people sought out mediums and fortune tellers during difficult times. At the height of the COVID-19 pandemic in 2020–21, the FBI and fraud helplines recorded an uptick in complaints about psychic crooks.

In February 2020, a New Jersey man visited a psychic in search of help with job troubles. He chose her after seeing positive reviews online. The young woman delivered a tarot-card reading and told him he had a curse that would hurt his family if he didn't do something about it quickly. The psychic offered to remove the curse if he brought her $9,000 in a pillowcase along with some roses and magnets.

Frightened by impending doom, the man used money he'd been saving for his son's college education and borrowed the rest from friends. He gave the psychic his $9,000, and she promised to abolish the curse. She assured him that after she succeeded in her cleansing ritual, he would get his money returned.

When he later asked for the cash, she wouldn't hand it over. Without evidence to prove what had happened, he couldn't convince the police to do anything. To make his situation worse, the man was laid off because of pandemic job cuts.

## EASY TO FOOL

It's hard to imagine that anyone would fall for these scams. But con artists are clever. They can spot a distressed person, and they skillfully exploit anxiety.

The psychic guarantees that the client's troubles will disappear with some special help. Because the fraudster seems to know personal details, the client believes that this psychic truly has supernatural powers to solve problems.

In 1925, Houdini stated that a medium could invent an impressive message from the spirits with just two or three details about the client. "Give a clever medium a man's name, address, and occupation," he said, "and with the aid of a few leading questions and a little deduction, the medium can convince that man that he knows the innermost secrets of his soul."

Deceiving customers today is far easier than it was a hundred years ago. An internet search provides dates, addresses, job histories, family connections, and much more. Many people lay out their lives on social media. When clients make an appointment for psychic services, they supply name and payment information. Armed with this background information, the psychics practice the "hot-reading technique," using the personal details to tell the future or give advice.

Without access to those facts, psychics observe the sitter, noting appearance, body language, voice. They fish for information just as the fake mediums did a century ago. For example, they might say, "I see someone with a name that starts with the letter J. Does that fit anyone in your life?" Or, "I see a woman with a flower garden. Does this make sense?"

If the sitter replies yes, the medium or psychic uses guesses and questions to zero in. Psychics know that most people come to them for help with their love life, financial questions, career, or health concerns. Based on a knowledge of human nature and these common issues, the medium makes general, vague comments that gullible sitters think apply perfectly to them.

A group gathers for a séance today in much the way the early spiritualists did in the nineteenth century. A Ouija board sits in the center of the table. With personal information widely available online, it's easier for fake psychics to dupe sitters than it was a century or more ago.

# PSYCHIC SCHOOL

Lily Dale, New York, is still the gathering place for mediums that it was when Houdini and Mackenberg exposed Pierre Keeler as a fraud in 1925. Calling itself "the world's largest center of the religion of Spiritualism," it welcomes 22,000 people every year, mostly in its summer season.

Visitors pay a gate fee to enter the village. The charge covers several large group events during which mediums deliver spirit messages. Private readings with mediums cost more.

The Lily Dale summer catalog advertises séances with trumpet levitation, ectoplasm, table tipping, and direct voice spirit messages.

Throughout the summer, workshops are available to learn how to give medium readings, practice spiritual healing, interpret dreams, read tarot cards, and more. Classes in mediumship are also available online.

Lily Dale emphasizes that its mediums are practicing a religion and are exempt from laws that forbid fortune-telling.

A medium's sign hangs outside her house in Lily Dale.

## EASY TO FIND

Supernatural and paranormal phenomena are familiar topics on social media, websites, and podcasts as well as in print, films, and television. Psychics and mediums write books and appear before large live audiences.

In addition to in-person and online readings, customers of psychics and mediums have the option of connecting by phone, email, text, video, app, or live chat. And they can do it 24/7. The charge is often several dollars per minute.

Perhaps all this exposure is why so many people in the United States believe in the supernatural. In polls conducted during the past twenty years, roughly 40 percent of Americans said that ghosts exist. Yet in a 1990 Gallup poll, only 25 percent of Americans reported believing in spirits.

A man seems to be surrounded by the ghosts of three children. This spirit photograph by William Mumler was created using trick photography during the 1860s or 1870s. Today, about four in ten Americans say they believe in ghosts.

A 2021 Pew Research Center survey found that 72 percent of US adults think it's possible to feel the presence of someone who has died. Nearly half those surveyed say that it's possible to communicate with the dead.

Harry Houdini pointed out that you don't have to be a spiritualist to expect a reunion with your family and friends in the afterlife. You don't need a medium to feel that your deceased loved ones are watching over you. But psychic crooks take advantage of those expectations and feelings to deceive and cheat. No supernatural ability is required to fool people who are ready to accept anything they're told.

In 1949, Rose Mackenberg said, "As long as people have troubles, fake mediums will have business!"

Spirit sleuths like Houdini, Mackenberg, and others set their sights on these swindlers. Today, magicians continue to expose fraudulent psychics and ruthless mediums by replicating supposedly mystical feats. The Society of American Magicians has a Paranormal Investigation Committee.

Other investigators check out and debunk claims of paranormal events such as ghost hauntings, quack medical cures, and mind reading. (See "Debunking the Supernatural" in More to Explore.)

In the end, though, it's up to individuals to think critically and be on guard so that they don't become another victim of a supernatural hoax.

Spirit photographs continued to be popular for decades. This one was taken in 1901 by a Chicago photographer. It shows the cut-out portraits of famous dead people hovering around a woman's head as if they were spirits.

# TIMELINE

| | |
|---|---|
| 1848 | Fox sisters report their ability to communicate with spirits. |
| 1855 | Davenport brothers start their touring careers. |
| **1861–1865** | **American Civil War.** |
| 1862 | William Mumler begins creating spirit photographs. |
| 1864–68 | Davenport brothers tour Europe. |
| 1865 | John Nevil Maskelyne discovers the Davenport Spirit Cabinet trick and begins using it in his magic show. |
| 1869 | Transcontinental Railroad completed. |
| | Harry Kellar becomes an assistant to the Davenport brothers. |
| 1873 | Harry Kellar establishes a magic program using the Spirit Cabinet. |
| 1874 March 24 | Ehrich Weiss, the future Harry Houdini, born in Budapest, Hungary. |
| 1884 | Seybert Commission investigates mediums. |
| 1888 | Maggie Fox Kane confesses to being a fraud. |
| 1892 July 10 | Rose Mackenberg born in New York. |
| **1914–18** | **The Great War, World War I.** |
| 1920 | Houdini and Conan Doyle meet and begin a correspondence. |
| 1922 | Houdini and Conan Doyle fall out over their different views about spiritualism. |
| 1923 | *Scientific American* offers a prize to a genuine medium. |
| 1924 | As a judge for the *Scientific American* contest, Houdini investigates the medium Margery. |
| 1925 | Rose Mackenberg works as an investigator for Houdini. |
| 1926 | |
| February & May | Houdini and Mackenberg testify before Congress about fraudulent mediums. |
| October 31 | Houdini dies from complications of a ruptured appendix. |
| 1927 | Mackenberg begins her thirty-year solo career as a ghostbuster. |
| 1936 | |
| October 31 | Bess Houdini holds her final séance to reach Harry Houdini. |
| **1939–1945** | **World War II.** |
| 1968 April 10 | Rose Mackenberg dies in New York. |

# GLOSSARY

**astrology:** the practice of predicting the future by studying the influence of stars and planets on people and events.

**automatic** or **spirit writing:** the supposed ability of a person in a trance to produce messages sent by a spirit.

**clairvoyant:** a person who claims to foretell the future or to see events, people, and objects that are not visible to others.

**conjuring:** performing magic.

**debunk:** to prove untrue or deceptive.

**ectoplasm:** a substance seeming to come from a medium's body that is said to be a spirit making itself visible to the living.

**fortune-telling:** predicting coming events, typically for money, by such methods as using cards, reading palms or tea leaves, gazing into a crystal ball, or being clairvoyant.

**ghost:** the spirit of a dead person that may appear in bodily form.

**manifestation:** the evidence that a spirit is present, revealed in a way that can be seen, heard, felt. Examples are rappings, speaking trumpets, tipping tables, and ectoplasm.

**materialization:** the act of a spirit assuming the bodily form of a human.

**medium:** a person who claims to contact spirits of dead people and enable communication with them.

**peritonitis:** inflammation of the lining of the abdomen and its organs caused by an infection.

**psychic:** a person who claims to have the ability to perceive information beyond the typical senses, making it possible to predict the future, read minds, or communicate with the dead.

**raps:** knocking sounds supposedly made by the spirits.

**séance:** a gathering at which people try to communicate with the spirits of the dead.

**sitter:** a person who attends a séance, usually after paying a fee.

**skeptic:** a person who suspects that a séance or other supernatural phenomenon is fake.

**spirit:** the essence of a living being that is said to leave the dead body and survive; a ghost.

**spirit guide:** the helper ghost that the medium claims assists in communications with those in the spirit world.

**spirit photography:** camera pictures that appear to show ghosts.

**spiritualism:** a belief that spirits of the dead communicate with the living, usually through a medium.

**supernatural,** or **paranormal:** something outside the observable physical world that can't be explained by known science.

**table tipping:** an occurrence during a séance when a table turns, tilts, or rises, allegedly due to a spirit's actions.

**tarot cards:** a special deck of cards used for fortune-telling.

**telepathy:** communication of thoughts without using the five senses; mind reading.

**trance:** a semiconscious, sleeplike daze state.

# MORE TO EXPLORE

## THE FOX SISTERS

Barb Rosenstock. *American Spirits*. New York: Calkins Creek, 2025.

Find out more about the Fox sisters in this biography for young readers.

## HARRY KELLAR

Gail Jarrow. *The Amazing Harry Kellar: Great American Magician*. Honesdale, PA: Calkins Creek, 2012.

Check out this biography of the famous American magician who began his career during the Civil War and entertained audiences until 1908. Discover how he learned spiritualist deceptions from the Davenport brothers and incorporated the tricks into his magic shows. Read about his friendship with Harry Houdini.

## HOUDINI

*American Experience*, "Houdini: The Man Behind the Myth."

PBS and WGBH Educational Foundation, 2000

**pbs.org/wgbh/americanexperience/films/ houdini/**

Find articles about Houdini's life and career; his escape secrets; his friendship with Sir Arthur Conan Doyle; and his exposure of the medium Margery. The transcript of the broadcast is also available.

*Houdini*

PBS Wisconsin Public Television Network, 1987

**pbs.org/video/wpt-documentaries-houdini/**

Watch a documentary about Houdini's life and career. See clips from Houdini's silent movies and performances. Listen to Houdini's niece recall her childhood living with her Uncle Harry and Aunt Bess. Be amazed as magician Doug Henning performs Metamorphosis in Appleton, Wisconsin, Houdini's boyhood home.

*Houdini 1936 Final Official Séance*

houdinimuseum

**youtube.com/watch?v=xnmY0kX8U6s**

Listen to an audio recording of Bess Houdini's last attempt to reach her late husband at a public séance on October 31, 1936. View a collection of Houdini photographs.

Houdini Archival Footage

David Folender

**youtube.com/watch?v=4ZX6NzOehKY**

Watch silent film clips of Houdini performing his escapes and stunts more than one hundred years ago.

Inside "Houdini: Art and Magic"—East Indian Needle Trick

Contemporary Jewish Museum, 2011

**youtube.com/watch?v=UL-pLZfYU6w**

Magician Joshua Jay discusses Houdini's famous trick and shows a display of the needles he once used.

Metamorphosis as performed by Hardeen

David Folender

**youtube.com/watch?v=97F8vryo8Sw**

Watch a silent film in which Houdini's brother Hardeen performs the illusion Metamorphosis made famous by Harry and Bess Houdini.

*This Dangerous Trick Wowed Houdini's Fans*

Smithsonian Channel, 2020

**youtube.com/watch?v=mbBF_3WbrRk**

Get a look at the Water Torture Cell escape and listen to a magician discuss how Houdini performed this death-defying stunt.

Houdini Museum Tour & Magic Show
Scranton, PA
**houdini.org**
A visit includes a tour of the museum's collection of Houdini memorabilia, film clips of the magician, and a live magic show.

## WEBSITES DEDICATED TO HOUDINI'S CAREER

John Cox
**wildabouthoudini.com**
This blog by Houdini historian John Cox is a treasure trove of information about Houdini's career and personal life.

Tom Interval
**intervalmagic.com/houdini**
The website by magician and magic historian Tom Interval has links to online sources about Houdini. Included are *New York Times* articles about the magician and his exploits beginning in 1910.

## TRICKS OF THE MEDIUMS
*Spirit Sleuths* explains only a few of the many ways that fake mediums performed deceptive séance effects. To learn others, check out these online sources from the nineteenth and early twentieth centuries.

Harry Houdini. *A Magician Among the Spirits*. New York: Harper & Brothers, 1924.
**archive.org/details/magicianamongspi00houd**

Julia E. Garrett. *Mediums Unmasked: An Exposé of Modern Spiritualism by an Ex-Medium*. Los Angeles: H. M. Lee & Bro., 1892.
**archive.org/details/mediumsunmaskede00garr**

*Revelations of a Spirit Medium*. Compiled by Harry Price and Eric J. Dingwall. New York: E. P. Dutton, 1922. Original edition, St. Paul, MN: Farrington & Co., 1891.
**archive.org/details/revelationsofspi00farriala**

## DEBUNKING THE SUPERNATURAL
Learn how modern-day magicians and investigators expose psychic fakes.

*Nova*, "Secrets of the Psychics"
PBS, 1993
**youtube.com/watch?v=abGzsT_Kmlk**
In this *Nova* episode, magician and psychic investigator James Randi, "the Amazing Randi," follows in Houdini's footsteps as he debunks reports of supernatural phenomena, including faith healing, palm-reading, astrology, spoon-bending, and psychic readings. A teacher's guide to the episode is available at:
"*Nova* Teacher's Guide: Secrets of the Psychics"
PBS, updated 2007.
**pbs.org/wgbh/nova/teachers/programs/2012_psychics.html**

"Why People Believe Weird Things"
Michael Shermer, publisher of *Skeptic* magazine and director of the Skeptic Society
*TED2006*
**ted.com/talks/michael_shermer_why_people_believe_weird_things**
In this TED Talk, Shermer explains why people are easily deceived. He reveals the truth behind several phenomena that have been called supernatural.

"Brain Magic"
Keith Barry
*TED2004*
**ted.com/talks/keith_barry_brain_magic**
During this TED Talk, magician Keith Barry performs surprising tricks that fool his audience. It's easy to think that he has supernatural power, but he's just a clever conjurer.

"Penn and Teller Reveal the Secret to Pulling Off a Mentalist Trick"
*Inside Edition*, 2016
**youtube.com/watch?v=gky1-Ji_ArQ**
Some psychics and mediums claim to have the mystical power to read minds. Watch several magicians demonstrate how mentalists accomplish this by using tricks and skill. Find out how to do a few of their tricks.

"Mentalism, Mind Reading and the Art of Getting Inside Your Head"
Derren Brown
*TED2019*
**ted.com/talks/derren_brown_mentalism_mind_reading_and_the_art_of_getting_inside_your_head**
Performer Derren Brown demonstrates sealed envelope reading, which mediums say is a sign of their psychic power. He declares that it's all a trick.

**Harry Houdini about 1909–10**

# AUTHOR'S NOTE

*Spirit Sleuths* is a cross between two of my previous books: *The Amazing Harry Kellar: Great American Magician* (2012) and *Spooked!* (2018). My research for those books brought me to the subject of ghost detectives and psychic frauds.

In writing about the world-renowned conjurer Kellar, I learned how he and other magic entertainers replicated séance manifestations in their performances. Near the end of Kellar's career, he developed a close friendship with Harry Houdini, who was twenty-five years younger. Reading about that relationship, I became aware of Houdini's efforts to expose fraudulent mediums using his magician's knowledge of séance tricks. That led me to Rose Mackenberg, a path-breaking woman ahead of her time as a ghost detective.

In *Spooked!*, I explored how the 1938 radio dramatization of H. G. Wells's novel *The War of the Worlds* convinced gullible listeners that Martians had invaded Earth. The book discussed the fallout after people unquestioningly believed what they heard on the radio. Like *Spooked!, Spirit Sleuths* reveals the importance of critical thinking.

When we attend a magic show, we know the magician is going to fool us. We enjoy being misled and tricked. Although magicians keep their methods secret, they never claim to use supernatural powers to wow and amaze us. But when people visit a medium to communicate with a dead loved one, they don't expect to be deceived. They're looking for comfort, not entertainment.

The spirit sleuths recognized the unfortunate consequences of grief colliding with greed. They tried to protect the public from swindlers and charlatans who took advantage of the most vulnerable.

As part of my research for this book, I dug into the lives and activities of the spotlighted spirit sleuths, relying on their own words whenever possible. Both Houdini and Mackenberg left behind extensive writings and interviews. I learned about séance scams from the work of magicians and reformed mediums.

To get a broad picture of spiritualism from the religion's early days to the present, I sought out the views of both its followers and critics. I gained more historical perspective by reading newspaper coverage of spiritualism from the mid-1800s through the 1900s.

When I write about a historical period, I usually can't physically step back into that world. But with this book, I was able to add personal experience to my research sources.

My encounters with spiritualism, mediums, and fortune tellers began when I was a child. Growing up in a small town, I knew older adults who were interested in spiritualism. These were members of mainstream Protestant churches. They were educated and sensible people. Yet spiritualism fascinated them as it did many of their generation who came of age in the shadow of a world war.

I overheard stories about a woman named Daisy. I was too young to pick up whether she was a medium or a fortune teller, but I knew there was a mystique about her. She collected clients by word of mouth only, and a friend had to provide directions to her house hidden somewhere out in the country. Daisy must have satisfied people because they kept going back for more.

The summer when I was eight, I was taken along on a day trip to a spiritualist camp in Ephrata, Pennsylvania. This was the same place that Rose Mackenberg and a newspaper reporter investigated in 1934 as part of their spiritualism exposé. (See chapter nine.) Their report hadn't permanently deterred visitors; I remember a full auditorium. A dynamic woman stood at the front pointing to people in the audience and sharing messages from their dead loved ones. Even as a child observer, I suspected there was a trick involved.

Decades later, I traveled to the spiritualist enclave of Lily Dale, New York, as part of my *Spirit Sleuths* research. The trip gave me a sense of the village where Houdini and Mackenberg exposed the famous medium Pierre Keeler. (See chapter seven.)

The crowds there were larger in the early 1900s. The buildings in the old photographs had fresher paint and appeared sturdier back then. But the mediums' techniques and messages were the same as those I had witnessed in Ephrata and had read about in accounts from the late nineteenth and early twentieth centuries.

When I started this book, I listened to an audiotape created for me thirty years ago by a fortune teller. I'd kept it all these years but hadn't listened to it since then. At the time, a psychic fair had come to the conference room of a local hotel. Out of curiosity, I had checked it out.

I paid a fee to a woman who read tarot cards. Although I didn't go to the extremes that Houdini and Mackenberg did in disguising myself or creating a false identity, I avoided volunteering any personal information. The woman probably deduced my age and other details from my physical appearance and dress. As she flipped over cards, she fished for clues. She made guesses and tried to verify them with me. I didn't lie, though I kept my answers a curt yes or no.

Absolutely nothing she told me about my future turned out to be correct. If I had taken it seriously and followed her advice, my life would have been very different . . . and not in a good way.

I wonder if others who attended that fair changed their lives because of a psychic message. What about people today who pay psychics for advice? Do they follow the guidance of a medium or fortune teller when they make important decisions? Do they regularly rely on a psychic's help in navigating life? How many choose a ruinous path by taking the word of a person who made it all up?

The true stories in this book show what can happen when people are not sufficiently skeptical. Misinformation, disinformation, bias, and propaganda permeate today's media and social interactions. Deep fakes and artificial intelligence can fool us. We have to be on guard against those who want to manipulate our beliefs and behavior for their own purposes. Perhaps these moments from history will encourage readers to question and analyze what they see and hear.

—GJ

# ACKNOWLEDGMENTS

I appreciate those who helped me along the way as I researched and wrote *Spirit Sleuths*. Many thanks to the following people for generously sharing their expertise and time:

John Cox, Houdini historian and chronologist at WildAboutHoudini.com—for contributing a wealth of information about Houdini, clearing up myths, and supplying research sources and photograph dates.

Tom Interval, magician, writer, and Houdini enthusiast at intervalmagic.com—for sharing his knowledge of Houdini and magic, suggesting resources, and giving a conjurer's perspective on today's fraudulent psychics.

Dorothy Dietrich, magician, escape artist, historian, and director of the Houdini Museum Tour & Magic Show—for providing her insight into Houdini's career and dishonest mediums.

Howard Blackwell, magician and mentalist—for answering my questions about the Needle Trick, which he performs, and about Houdini's needles, a set of which he owns.

Barb Rosenstock, author of the forthcoming *American Spirits* (Calkins Creek) and *Houdini's Library* (Knopf)—for helping me make sense of the many contradictions surrounding the Fox sisters and for passing along tips about researching Houdini.

Cornell University's library staff—for assisting me with printed resources.

I'm grateful to my husband, Robert, for accompanying me on field trips and for commenting as I read the first draft of each chapter aloud so that I could hear the flow of the words.

As with all my books, I feel fortunate to have received the support and encouragement of my longtime editor, Carolyn P. Yoder, and the contributions of the talented and dedicated team at Calkins Creek/Astra Books for Young Readers.

—GJ

# SOURCE NOTES

The source of each quotation in this book is found below. The citation indicates the first words of the quotation and its document source. The sources are listed either in the bibliography or below. (Websites are active at time of publication.)

The following abbreviations for bibliography entries are used:

AMATS—Harry Houdini, *A Magician Among the Spirits*

Hearings—U.S. Congress. House of Representatives. Subcommittee on Judiciary of the Committee on the District of Columbia

Seybert—*Preliminary Report of the Commission Appointed by the University of Pennsylvania to Investigate Modern Spiritualism, in Accordance with the Request of the Late Henry Seybert*

## CHAPTER ONE
## A VISIT WITH GHOSTS

"I there witnessed . . .": Edmonds and Dexter, p. 26.

## CHAPTER TWO
## SPEAKING TO THE DEAD

"They came . . .": Hardinge, p. 39.

"Is this a human being . . ." and "Is it a spirit . . .": Mrs. Fox, quoted in Underhill, p. 7.

"her peculiar powers . . .": advertisement, *New-York Daily Tribune*, December 30, 1856.

"complexions of . . .": "City Items: An Hour with 'The Spirits,'" *New-York Daily Tribune*, June 5, 1850.

"Are you a relative?" and "How many years . . .": quoted in same as above.

"not willing to believe . . .": "City Items: An Hour with 'The Spirits,'" same as above.

"We found our so-called . . .": Britten, p. 555.

"comforts the mourner . . ." and "smooths the passage . . .": Edmonds and Dexter, p. 78.

"a young, innocent . . .": Edmonds and Dexter, p. 16.

"Mourn no more . . ." and "he lives . . .": letter from H. Link to Mr. and Mrs. Keller, Little Falls, NY, June 6, 1852, quoted in Cox, p. 84.

"pretended answers . . ." and "Spiritual Knockings": "Lectures on Imagination," *Sunday [NY] Dispatch*, January 12, 1851.

"No rational mind . . .": same as above.

"It is most surprising . . .": *Philadelphia North American*, quoted in "Here's a Knocking. Indeed—Knock, knock, knock: Who's there i' the name of Beelzebub!", *Indiana State Sentinel*, July 11, 1850.

## CHAPTER THREE
## ABRACADABRA

"Medium and conjuror . . .": Maskelyne, p. 174.

"super-human power.": AMATS, p. 26.

"to indicate that they . . .": Cooper, p. 215.

"I got a key . . .": Maskelyne, p. 66.

"There does not . . ." and "a professed . . .": Weatherly and Maskelyne, p. 183.

"the Brothers did . . .": Maskelyne, p. 65.

"Make a bold front . . .": quoted in "Spiritualism at the White House," *Cleveland Morning Leader*, June 4, 1863.

"Tell us when . . .": same as above.

"Concentrate your forces . . .": same as above.

"Their talk and advices . . .": same as above.

"Never in any period . . .": Hardinge, p. 509.

"There was one chance . . .": quoted in AMATS, p. 22.

## CHAPTER FOUR
## SUSPICIOUS SÉANCES

"What fools are they . . .": quoted in Davenport, p. 235.

"I see now . . ." and "although when . . .": Mrs. Knight, quoted in Johnson, 320.

"The most severe . . .": Hardinge, p. 247.

"solely on our . . .": Seybert, p. 5.

"fraudulent throughout. There was . . .": Seybert p. 7.

"Is he satisfied . . .": Seybert, p. 33.

"I will be satisfied . . .": Seybert, p. 34.

"so-called raps . . .": letter from Horace Howard
    Furness to George Fullerton, November 7, 1884,
    in Seybert, p. 48.

"unsatisfactory.": quoted in same as above.

"In only two instances . . .": H. H. Furness, Seybert,
    p. 150.

"I have been forced . . .": George Fullerton,
    Seybert, p. 26.

"the darkened . . .": H. H. Furness, Seybert, p 151.

"There is no doubt . . .": Doyle, Vol. 1, p. 325.

"far more remarkable . . .": Seybert, pp. 20–21.

"received its most . . .": Weatherly and Maskelyne,
    p. 214.

"Spiritualism is a curse.": letter from Margaret F.
    Kane to editor of the New York Herald, May 14,
    1888, in Davenport, p. 30.

"After my sister Katie . . ." and "I never believed
    . . .": statement published in New York World,
    reprinted in "How the Spirits Knocked," Evening
    Star [DC], October 22, 1888.

"just for the fun . . .": quoted in Davenport, p. 92.

"it was the spirits . . .": same as above.

"We were too young . . .": quoted in Davenport, 93.

"So many persons . . ." and "that we could not . . .":
    quoted in Davenport, p. 92.

"I do not exaggerate . . .": quoted in Davenport,
    p. 232.

"is all a fraud, . . .": statement published in
    New York World, reprinted in "How the Spirits
    Knocked," Evening Star [DC], October 22, 1888.

"I am now eighty-one . . .": letter from E. F. Bunnell
    to Margaret Fox Kane, October 2, 1888,
    Davenport, p. 70.

"Their revelations . . .": quoted in "Discrediting
    the Fox Sisters," Evening Star [DC], October 22,
    1888.

"Spiritualism's Downfall": Morning News
    [Savannah, GA], October 24, 1888.

"A Spiritualistic Expose.": Omaha [NE] Daily Bee,
    October 22, 1888.

"the most heartless . . .": Garrett, p. 14.

"a death blow . . .": "Spiritualism's Downfall,"
    Morning News [Savannah, GA], October 24,
    1888.

"I know there are . . ." and "and I feel sorry . . .":
    Garrett, Mediums Unmasked, p. 8.

"No medium believes . . .": Garrett, Mediums
    Unmasked, p. 11.

"Spiritualistic impostors . . .": "The Spiritualistic
    Humbug," Evening World [NY], October 22,
    1888.

## CHAPTER FIVE
## THE MAGICIAN AND THE SPIRITUALIST

"I saw my dead . . .": letter from Conan Doyle to
    Houdini, summer 1920, in Ernst and Carrington,
    p. 128.

"She was stabbed . . .": quoted in Kalush and
    Sloman, p. 48. Based on Dorothy Kipper
    Lickteig, Anderson County Kansas Early
    Gleanings, Anderson County Historical Society,
    n.d.

"Was the killer . . .": same as above.

"No.": same as above.

"So he was known . . .": same as above.

"Yes.": same as above.

"What is the murderer's name?" and "His name."
    and "Answer!": quoted in Kalush and Sloman,
    p. 49. Based on Dorothy Kipper Lickteig,
    Anderson County Kansas Early Gleanings,
    Anderson County Historical Society, n.d.

"His name is . . .": same as above.

"The people were so . . .": quoted in Kellock,
    p. 109.

"the greatest sensational . . .": Houdini poster for
    the Water Torture Cell.

"I do not dematerialize . . .": quoted in Kellock,
    p. 15.

"were performed as the . . .": quoted in Kellock,
    pp. 13–14.

"It is all hocus-pocus." Houdini, in Hearings,
    May 20, 1926, p. 71.

"that the Davenport . . .": letter from Houdini to
    Conan Doyle, March 17, 1920, in Ernst and
    Carrington, p. 45.

"I promise to go . . .": letter from Houdini to Conan
    Doyle, April 1920, in Ernst and Carrington,
    p. 88.

"the most important thing . . .": Conan Doyle, *Memories and Adventures*, p. 390.

"She has her off-days, as . . .": letter from Conan Doyle to Houdini, April 5, 1920, in Ernst and Carrington, p. 121.

"In his great mind . . .": AMATS, p. 138.

"Mene, mene, . . .": Ernst and Carrington, p. 243.

"I won't tell you . . .": same as above.

"Mediums are all fakers.": Francis Martinka quoted in Rinn, p. 22.

## CHAPTER SIX
## THE SPOOK HUNT

"I do not say . . .": "Houdini on Spiritualism," letter from Houdini to editor, printed in *New York Times*, July 5, 1922.

"Oh, my darling, . . ." and "I've tried . . .": quoted in AMATS, p. 153.

"God bless . . ." and "for what you . . .": quoted in AMATS, p. 154.

"I felt rather . . .": letter from Conan Doyle to Houdini, November 19, 1922, in Ernst and Carrington, p. 167.

"Up to the present . . .": letter from Houdini to Conan Doyle, December 15, 1922, in Ernst and Carrington, p. 169.

"It is quite . . ." and "to invent . . .": Joseph Jastrow, "The Logic of Mental Telegraphy," *Scribner's Magazine*, Vol. 18 (November 1895), p. 576.

"As conjuring-tricks . . .": William Marriott, "On the Edge of the Unknown: Spirit Messages," *Pearson's Magazine*, Vol. 29 (April 1910), p. 364.

"I am not surprised . . .": quoted in James C. Young, "Magic and Mediums."

"Views of conjurers . . ." and "are generally . . .": Arthur Conan Doyle, "Letter from Mother Presented to Houdini," *Galveston* [TX] *Daily News*, October 30, 1922.

"A large money reward . . ." and "while the best . . .": letter from Conan Doyle to Editor, *Scientific American*, January 1923, p. 57.

"gentle, quiet, . . .": same as above.

"It seems that . . .": Arthur Brisbane, "Today," *Omaha* [NE] *Morning Bee*, August 30, 1924.

"There is no assurance . . .": quoted in "Positive and Negative Proofs Result from Psychic Tests," *Evening Star* [DC], August 28, 1924.

"came with his mind . . .": L. R. G. Crandon, "The Margery Mediumship, Experiments in Psychic Science," in Murchison, p. 78.

"this low-minded . . .": letter from L. R. G. Crandon to Arthur Conan Doyle, quoted in Silverman, p. 325.

"the famous Margery case . . .": "The Psychic Investigation," *Scientific American*, April 1925, p. 229.

"Everything which took place . . .": "Statement by Houdini," August 28, 1924, in E. E. Free, editor, "Our Psychic Investigation," *Scientific American*, November 1924, p. 304.

"I am convinced . . .": "Statement by Hereward Carrington," August 29, 1924, in E. E. Free, editor, "Our Psychic Investigation," *Scientific American*, November 1924, p. 304.

"his preposterous . . .": Conan Doyle, *The History of Spiritualism*, Vol. 2, p. 219.

"Most people who go . . .": quoted in James C. Young, "Magic and Mediums."

## CHAPTER SEVEN
## UNDERCOVER AGENTS

"I do believe . . .": AMATS, p. 165.

"Where is mamma?": quoted in "Spiritualist Cult Blamed for Death in Nebraska Town," *New York World,* April 20, 1923.

"Mamma's in another . . .": same as above.

"We will soon . . .": same as above.

"friend Light . . .": same as above.

"tricksters and . . .": Houdini, "How I Unmask the Spirit Fakers," p. 153.

"Even the best . . .": and "The higher these . . .": Father C. M. de Heredia, quoted in "Spiritualism Is Taken Too Seriously Nowadays," *Buffalo* [NY] *Sunday Times*, March 11, 1923.

"Dear Julie, Dear . . .": quoted in George Britt, "Famous Slate Writer Is Unmasked by Womans Wit," *Americus* [GA] *Times-Recorder*, November 4, 1925.

"I've tried . . ." and "and now I've got . . .": same as above.

"I never would try . . .": same as above.

"That's a lie, an . . .": quoted by Mackenberg in "I've Unmasked a Thousand Frauds," p. 103.

"Not quite clear, but . . .": "'Divine Healer' Fails in Houdini Test; Names Police Chief as 'March 30, 1864,'" *Evening Star* [DC], September 18, 1925.

"What was the name . . .": same as above.

"Is it possible?" and "Who taught me . . .": same as above.

"anything which has convinced . . .": AMATS, p. 165.

"I have never received . . .": quoted in James C. Young, "Magic and Mediums."

"With Spirit photography . . ." and "there has never . . .": AMATS, p. 136.

## CHAPTER EIGHT
## CAPITAL SPIRITS

"Do not forget . . .": Houdini, "Houdini Jeers 'Spirit' Seers Who Claim Eerie Powers," *Brooklyn* [NY] *Daily Times*, January 23, 1926.

"Washington is the only . . .": Hearings, February 26, 1926, p. 15.

"I have examined . . .": Hearings, February 26, 1926, p. 7.

"They have not got . . .": Hearings, February 26, 1926, p. 15.

"Millions of dollars . . .": Hearings, May 18, 1926, p. 23.

"A fraudulent medium . . .": Hearings, May 18, 1926, p. 26.

"I do not believe . . ." and "They can not . . .": Hearings, May 18, 1926, p. 24.

"Almost all the . . .": Marcia, quoted in Hearings, May 18, 1926, p. 33.

"I know for a fact . . ." and "I have a number of . . .": Coates, quoted in Hearings, May 18, 1926, p. 33.

"Liar!": quoted in "Hints of Seances at White House," *New York Times*, May 19, 1926.

"crooks and criminals.": quoted in "Medium Denies She Reported Table Tippings at White House," *Evening Star* [DC], May 18, 1926.

"Your plans are . . .": quoted in "Hints of Seances at White House," *New York Times*, May 19, 1926.

"Hello, Edith Rogers.": same as above.

"shock, frighten . . .": Rose Mackenberg, "Houdini's Aide Says Six $25 Fees Bought Her Six Licenses to 'Marry and to Bury.'"

"quiet-mannered" and "soft-voiced.": Thomas L. Stokes, "'Not Interested,' Say Coolidges of Spiritualism," *Atlanta Constitution*, May 19, 1926.

"under the shadow . . .": Coates, quoted in "Hints of Seances at White House," *New York Times*, May 19, 1926.

"The President's cool . . .": "This Charge Can't Be True," *New York Times*, May 20, 1926.

"That money belongs . . .": Hearings, May 20, 1926, p. 67.

"He is demonstrating . . .": Hearings, May 20, 1926, p. 72.

"In my mind," and "I was thinking . . .": Hearings, May 20, 1926, pp. 75–76.

"My religion and . . .": Hearings, May 20, 1926, p. 51.

"reduced materially . . .": quoted in Brown, p. 154.

"I'm tired of fighting . . .": quoted in Kellock, p. 383.

"old Father Time . . .": William Burr, quoted in "Declares Harry Houdini Has at Last Discovered There Is a Spirit World," *Elmira* [NY] *Star-Gazette*, November 1, 1926.

"There is, after . . .": letter from Arthur Conan Doyle to Beatrice Houdini, January 23, 1927, in Ernst and Carrington, p. 217.

"Almost all mediums . . .": Conrad Hauser, quoted in "Spiritualists Claim Houdini as Medium," *Boston Daily Globe*, November 3, 1926.

"I hope now . . .": John Heiss, quoted in same as above.

"Houdini could escape . . ." and "If he cannot . . .": Bess Houdini quoted in "Wife Leads Attempt to Bring Back Ghost of Houdini," *Post-Press* [El Centro, CA], November 1, 1936.

"Houdini, are you . . ." and "We have waited, Houdini . . ." and "Come through, Harry!": Edward Saint, *Houdini 1936 Final Official Séance*, HoudiniMuseum, YouTube, *youtube. com/watch?v=xnmY0kX8U6s* at 10:19 and 10:39 and 12:49.

"Houdini did not . . ." and "I do not believe . . ." and "It is finished. Good . . .": Bess Houdini, *Houdini 1936 Final Official Séance*, HoudiniMuseum, YouTube, *youtube.com/ watch?v=xnmY0kX8U6s* at 14:05 and 14:11 and 14:46.

## CHAPTER NINE
### THE WOMAN WITH A THOUSAND HUSBANDS

"All they ever say . . .": quoted in Welshimer.

"My secret service . . ." and "Self-control . . .": Mackenberg, "Spiritualism, Possibly True, and 'Spiritualism' Demonstrably False."

"Houdini's Chief . . .": Mackenberg, "Houdini's Aide Says Six $25 Fees Bought Her Six Licenses to 'Marry and to Bury.'"

"I've received so many . . ." and "that I'm . . ." and "he's always . . .": quoted in E. W. Williamson, "A Lady with 36 Spirit Hubbies Says It's Fraud."

"I am watching over . . .": quoted in Mackenberg, "I've Unmasked a Thousand Frauds," p. 103.

"Spend it any way . . ." and "except that I . . .": same as above.

"I'm just trying . . ." and "So can I but . . .": quoted in Ruth Arell, "Spirits Are Easily Fooled By Some Disguises, She Finds," *Baltimore Sun*, May 25, 1941.

"I smell a rat . . .": quoted in Phyllis Battelle, "Miss Mackenberg Is Only Woman 'Ghost Buster,'" *Deseret News* [Salt Lake City, UT], December 25, 1949.

"I have never . . .": quoted in Ruth Arell, "Spirits Are Easily Fooled By Some Disguises, She Finds," *Baltimore Sun*, May 25, 1941.

"former husbands . . .": Mackenberg, "They Gave Me 1,500 Husbands," p. 55.

"a three-ring circus . . .": Mac Parker, "Ephrata Spiritualist Camp Revealed as 'Three-Ring Circus of Flim-Flam,'" *Lancaster* [PA] *New Era*, September 6, 1934.

"has for many years . . .": Zay Crossley, quoted in "Another Exposure Exposed," *Psychic News*, November 24, 1934.

"She would make . . .": "'Exposure' Bunk," *Psychic News*, September 11, 1937.

"The anguish . . ." and "offers a fertile . . .": Mackenberg, "I've Unmasked a Thousand Frauds," p. 26.

"mean and contemptible.": Mackenberg, "When Crime Poses as Spiritualism," March 12, 1939.

"Phantoms and Fakes.": "Clubwomen to Hear Expert on Fabrics," *Lancaster* [PA] *Sunday News*, September 7, 1952.

"Debunking the Ghost Racket." "Houdini Ex-Aide 'Debunks' Ghosts," *Brooklyn* [NY] *Daily Eagle*, June 18, 1946.

"My ghosts have . . .": quoted in John Cameron Swayze, "New York," *Lansing* [MI] *State Journal*, February 25, 1952.

"a female Sherlock Holmes.": "Radio," *Austin* [TX] *American*, April 5, 1941.

"1500 husbands, 3000 . . .": Mackenberg, "I've Unmasked a Thousand Frauds," p. 27.

"It's really awful . . ." and "I'd love . . .": quoted in Claire Cox, "Disappointed U.S. Spook-Hunter About Set to Give Up the Ghost," *Tyler* [TX] *Morning Telegraph*, April 12, 1949.

"The repeated disappointments . . ." and "caused her . . .": Sullivan, p. 146.

"we've no hope . . .": Sullivan, p. 157.

## CHAPTER TEN
### THE SUPERNATURAL RACKET

"When the spirits come in . . .": Rose Mackenberg, quoted in E. W. Williamson, "A Lady with 36 Spirit Hubbies Says It's Fraud."

"You've got to admit . . .": quoted in Houdini, "How I Unmask the Spirit Fakers," p. 152.

"If they are taking . . .": Celia Mitchell, quoted in
    Michael Wilson, "Seeing Freedom in Their
    Future, Psychics Reveal All: 'It's a Scam,'"
    *New York Times*, August 29, 2015.
"Give a clever . . ." and "and with the aid . . .":
    Houdini, "How I Unmask the Spirit Fakers,"
    p. 155.
"the world's largest . . .": Lily Dale Assembly,
    lilydaleassembly.org/frequently-asked-questions.
"As long as people have . . .": Rose Mackenberg,
    quoted in Phyllis Battelle, "Miss Mackenberg
    Is Only Woman 'Ghost Buster,'" *Deseret News*
    [Salt Lake City, UT], December 25, 1949.

Rose Mackenberg in
disguise, in 1937.

# BIBLIOGRAPHY

*Indicates a primary source

"America's Interesting People: Disguise." *American Magazine*, Vol. 123 (June 1937): 130.

Blum, Deborah. *Ghost Hunters: William James and the Search for Scientific Proof of Life After Death*. New York: Penguin Press, 2006.

Brandon, Ruth. *The Life and Many Deaths of Harry Houdini*. New York: Random House, 1993.

———. *The Spiritualists: The Passion for the Occult in the Nineteenth and Twentieth Centuries*. New York: Alfred A. Knopf, 1983.

Braude, Ann. *Radical Spirits: Spiritualism and Women's Rights in Nineteenth-Century America*, 2nd ed. Bloomington: Indiana University Press, 2001.

*Britten, Emma Hardinge. *Nineteenth Century Miracles; or, Spirits and Their Work in Every Country of the Earth: A Complete Historical Compendium of the Great Movement Known as "Modern Spiritualism."* New York: William Britten, 1884.

Brown, Raymond J. "The Most Mysterious Man in the World." *Popular Science Monthly*, October 1925: 16–17, 154–57.

Caveney, Mike, and Bill Miesel. *Kellar's Wonders*. Pasadena, CA: Mike Caveney's Magic Words, 2003.

Cep, Casey. "Kindred Spirits." *New Yorker*, Vol. 97 (May 31, 2021).

Christopher, Milbourne. *Houdini: The Untold Story*. New York: Thomas Y. Crowell, 1969.

Conan Doyle, Arthur. *The History of Spiritualism*, 2 vols. New York: George H. Doran, 1926.

*———. *Memories and Adventures*. Boston: Little, Brown, 1924.

*Cooper, Robert. *Spiritual Experiences, Including Seven Months with the Brothers Davenport*. London: Heywood & Co., 1867.

Copperfield, David, Richard Wiseman, and David Britland. *David Copperfield's History of Magic*. New York: Simon & Schuster, 2021.

Cox, Robert S. *Body and Soul: A Sympathetic History of American Spiritualism*. Charlottesville: University of Virginia Press, 2003.

Creekmore, Don. "Anniversary of Houdini's Visit to Garnett Noted as Moment of Change for Famous Performer." *Anderson County* [KS] *Review*, November 23, 2021.

Davenport, Reuben Briggs. *The Death-Blow to Spiritualism: Being the True Story of the Fox Sisters, as Revealed by Authority of Margaret Fox Kane and Catherine Fox Jencken*. 1888. Reprint, New York: Arno Press, 1976.

Dunninger, Joseph. *Houdini's Spirit Exposés from Houdini's Own Manuscripts, Recordings, and Photographs*. New York: Experimenter Publishing, 1928.

Dyson, Erika White. "Spiritualism and Crime: Negotiating Prophecy and Police Power at the Turn of the Twentieth Century." PhD diss., Columbia University, 2010.

*Edmonds, John W., and George T. Dexter. *Spiritualism*, 7th ed. New York: Partridge and Brittan, 1853.

Ernst, Bernard M. L., and Hereward Carrington. *Houdini and Conan Doyle: The Story of a Strange Friendship*. New York: Albert and Charles Boni, 1932.

*Fawkes, F. Attfield. *Spiritualism Exposed*. Bristol, England: J. W. Arrowsmith, 1920.

Foster, Freling. "Keep Up with the World." *Collier's*, Vol. 124 (December 31, 1949): 63.

*Garrett, Julia E. *Mediums Unmasked: An Exposé of Modern Spiritualism by an Ex-Medium*. Los Angeles: H. M. Lee & Bro., 1892.

Gresham, William Lindsay. *Houdini: The Man Who Walked Through Walls*. New York: Henry Holt, 1959.

*Hardinge, Emma. *Modern American Spiritualism: A Twenty Years' Record of the Communion Between Earth and the World of Spirits*, 2nd ed. New York: Emma Hardinge, 1870.

*Houdini. *Houdini Exposes the Tricks Used by the Boston Medium "Margery" to Win the $2500 Prize Offered by the Scientific American*. New York: Adams Press, 1924.

*———. "How I Do My 'Spirit Tricks." *Popular Science Monthly*, December 1925: 12–13, 150–55.

*———. "How I Unmask the Spirit Fakers." *Popular Science Monthly*, November 1925: 12–14, 152–56.

*———. *A Magician Among the Spirits*. New York: Harper & Brothers, 1924.

Houdini, Harry. Collection. Rare Book and Special Collections Division, Library of Congress, Washington, DC.

*———. *The Right Way to Do the Wrong: An Exposé of Successful Criminals*. Boston: self-published, 1906.

*———. *The Unmasking of Robert-Houdin*. New York: Publishers Printing, 1908.

Jaher, David. *The Witch of Lime Street: Séance, Seduction, and Houdini in the Spirit World*. New York: Broadway Books, 2015.

Johnson, Brandon LaVell. "Spirits on the Stage: Public Mediums, Spiritualist Theater, and American Culture, 1848–1893." Vol. 1. PhD diss., University of Chicago, 2007.

Kalush, William, and Larry Sloman. *The Secret Life of Houdini: The Making of America's First Superhero*. New York: Atria, 2006.

Kellock, Harold. *Houdini: His Life-Story from the Recollections and Documents of Beatrice Houdini*. New York: Harcourt, Brace, 1928.

*Kimbrough, Mary. "$5 Spiritualism Course Offered to Reporter." *St. Louis Star and Times*, July 12, 1945.

*———. "Imaginary Spirit at Séance Shuns Imaginary Problem." *St. Louis Star and Times*, July 14, 1945.

*———. "Many Fake Mediums Found to Employ Mechanical Devices to Victimize Gullible." *St. Louis Star and Times*, July 17, 1945.

*———. "'Pat,' 'Doc,' 'Running Wolf' and Reporter's Nonexistent Husband All Take the Stage." *St. Louis Star and Times*, July 16, 1945.

*———. "'Spirit' Wires Crossed on Imaginary Husband." *St. Louis Star and Times*, July 13, 1945.

*———. "War Bereaved Being Victimized." *St. Louis Star and Times*, July 11, 1945.

Lawton, George. *The Drama of Life After Death: A Study of the Spiritualist Religion*. New York: Henry Holt, 1932.

Loxton, Daniel. "Ghostbuster Girls!" *Junior Skeptic*, No. 46 (2013): 65–73.

———. "A Rare and Beautiful Thing." *Skeptic* magazine, Vol. 19 (2014): 26–32.

*Mackenberg, Rose. "Blasé Old London Proves Happy Hunting Ground for Suave Seeresses Who Thrive on Credulity." *Winnipeg Evening Tribune*, Magazine Section, March 23, 1929.

*———. "Dwarf Inside 'Psychic' Drum Causes Expose of Myra's Mesmeric Music." *Winnipeg Evening Tribune*, Magazine Section, March 16, 1929.

*———. "Exposing the Weird Secrets of 'Mediums' and Spirits." *Minneapolis Sunday Tribune*, May 12, 1929.

*———. "Houdini's Aide Says Six $25 Fees Bought Her Six Licenses to 'Marry and to Bury.'" *Winnipeg Evening Tribune*, Magazine Section, March 9, 1929.

*———. *Houdini's "Girl Detective": The Real-Life Ghost-Busting Adventures of Rose Mackenberg*. Compiled and introduced by Tony Wolf. Middletown, DE: CreateSpace Independent Publishing Platform, 2016.

*———. "Incredible Graft in Sale of Magic Charms Amulets and 'Love Philtres,' Is Revealed." *Winnipeg Evening Tribune*, Magazine Section, March 30, 1929.

*———. "Many Spiritualists Claimed Houdini Had Power to Enter Fourth Plane, Dissolving Material Body." *Winnipeg Evening Tribune*, Magazine Section, April 6, 1929.

*———. "Millionaire 'Medium' Rejects Houdini's $10,000 Challenge That He'll Duplicate 'Feats' By Magic." *Winnipeg Evening Tribune*, Magazine Section, April 13, 1929.

*———. "Mystic Cameras Dupe Bereaved with Fascinating Facts About Ectoplasm." *Winnipeg Evening Tribune*, Magazine Section, March 2, 1929.

*———. "Spiritualism, Possibly True, and 'Spiritualism' Demonstrably False." *Winnipeg Evening Tribune*, Magazine Section, February 23, 1929.

*———. "They Gave Me 1,500 Husbands." *American Magazine*, Vol. 131 (February 1941): 42–43, 54–55.

*———. "When Crime Poses as Spiritualism." *American Weekly*, a Sunday supplement, from *Pittsburgh Sun-Telegraph*, March 12 and March 19, 1939.

*Mackenberg, Rose (as told to Joseph Fulling Fishman). "I've Unmasked a Thousand Frauds." *Saturday Evening Post*, Vol. 223 (March 3, 1951): 26–27, 103–05.

Manseau, Peter. *The Apparitionists: A Tale of Phantoms, Fraud, Photography, and the Man Who Captured Lincoln's Ghost*. Boston: Houghton Mifflin Harcourt, 2017.

*Marriott, William. "On the Edge of the Unknown." *Pearson's Magazine*, Vol. 29 (March, April, May, June 1910): 236–46, 356–69, 509–21, 607–17.

*Maskelyne, John Nevil. *Modern Spiritualism: A Short Account of Its Rise and Progress, with Some Exposures of So-Called Spirit Media*. London: Frederick Warne, 1876.

McCabe, Joseph. *Is Spiritualism Based on Fraud?: The Evidence Given by Sir A. C. Doyle and Others Drastically Examined*. London: Watts & Co., 1920.

McManus-Young Collection, Library of Congress, Washington, DC.

Morton, Lisa. *Calling the Spirits: A History of Seances*. London: Reaktion Books, 2020.

*Mumler, William H. *The Personal Experiences of William H. Mumler in Spirit-Photography*. Boston: Colby and Rich, 1875.

Murchison, Carl, ed. *The Case For and Against Psychical Belief*. Worcester, MA: Clark University, 1927.

Natale, Simone. *Supernatural Entertainments: Victorian Spiritualism and the Rise of Modern Media Culture*. University Park: Pennsylvania State University Press, 2016.

*Nelson, Ralph. "Debunkers Dream Up Spirits." *Detroit Free Press*, August 9, 1945.

*———. "'Mediums' Operating Wide Open." *Detroit Free Press*, August 10, 1945.

*———. "'Mediums' Raking In $1,000,000." *Detroit Free Press*, August 6, 1945.

*———. "Specialty of Medium Is Solace." *Detroit Free Press*, August 7, 1945.

*———. "Spirits Garner Fat Fees as 'Physicians.'" *Detroit Free Press*, August 8, 1945.

Nichols, T. L. *A Biography of the Brothers Davenport*. London: Saunders, Otley and Co., 1864.

Nickell, Joe. "Role-Playing Detectives and the Paranormal." *Skeptical Inquirer*, Vol. 45 (July/August 2021).

———. *The Science of Ghosts: Searching for Spirits of the Dead*. Amherst, NY: Prometheus Books, 2012.

Oppenheim, Janet. *The Other World: Spiritualism and Psychical Research in England, 1850–1914*. Cambridge, UK: Cambridge University Press, 1985.

Polidoro, Massimo. *Final Séance: The Strange Friendship Between Houdini and Conan Doyle*. Amherst, NY: Prometheus Books, 2001.

*Preliminary Report of the Commission Appointed by the University of Pennsylvania to Investigate Modern Spiritualism, in Accordance with the Request of the Late Henry Seybert*. Philadelphia: J. B. Lippincott, 1887.

Price, Harry. *Fifty Years of Psychical Research: A Critical Survey*. 1939. Reprint, New York: Arno Press, 1975.

*Price, Harry, and Eric J. Dingwall, compilers. *Revelations of a Spirit Medium.* New York: E. P. Dutton, 1922. Original edition, St. Paul, MN: Farrington & Co., 1891.

*Proskauer, Julien J. *Spook Crooks!: Exposing the Secrets of the Prophet-eers Who Conduct Our Wickedest Industry.* New York: A. L. Burt, 1932.

Ptacin, Mira. *The In-Betweens: The Spiritualists, Mediums, and Legends of Camp Etna.* New York: Liveright Publishing, 2019.

Randi, James. *An Encyclopedia of Claims, Frauds, and Hoaxes of the Occult and Supernatural.* New York: St. Martin's Press, 1995.

———. *Flim-Flam: Psychics, ESP, Unicorns and Other Delusions.* Buffalo, NY: Prometheus Books, 1982.

*Rinn, Joseph F. *Searchlight on Psychical Research.* London: Rider and Company, 1954.

Roach, Mary. *Spook: Science Tackles the Afterlife.* New York: W. W. Norton, 2005.

Sandford, Christopher. *Houdini and Conan Doyle.* London: Duckworth Overlook, 2011.

Schwartz, Stephan A. "Spirit World." *American Heritage*, Vol. 56 (April/May 2005).

Silverman, Kenneth. *Houdini!!!: The Career of Ehrich Weiss.* New York: HarperCollins, 1996.

Steinmeyer, Jim. *Hiding the Elephant: How Magicians Invented the Impossible and Learned to Disappear.* New York: Carroll & Graf, 2003.

*Sullivan, Mary. *My Double Life: The Story of a New York Policewoman.* New York: Farrar & Rinehart, 1938.

Tompkins, Matthew L. *The Spectacle of Illusion: Magic, the Paranormal and the Complicity of the Mind.* London: Thames and Hudson, 2019.

*Underhill, A. Leah. *The Missing Link in Modern Spiritualism.* New York: Thomas R. Knox, 1885.

*U.S. Congress. House of Representatives. Subcommittee on Judiciary of the Committee on the District of Columbia. *Fortune Telling: Hearings on H. R. 8989*, Sixty-Ninth Congress, First session, February 26, May 18, 20, and 21, 1926.

Weatherly, Lionel A., and J. N. Maskelyne. *The Supernatural?* Bristol and London: J. W. Arrowsmith, 1891.

Weisberg, Barbara M, "They Spoke With the Dead." *American Heritage*, Vol. 50 (September 1999).

Welshimer, Helen. "Made a Frump out of Herself to Expose the Fake Mediums." *Arizona Republic*, August 15, 1937.

*Williamson, E. W. "Crinkle of Bills and Tinkle of Coins Spur Spirits' Ardor." *Chicago Daily Tribune*, August 6, 1945.

*———. "A Lady with 36 Spirit Hubbies Says It's Fraud." *Chicago Daily Tribune*, August 9, 1945.

*———. "Spirit Fakers of City Fatten on War Grief." *Chicago Daily Tribune*, August 5, 1945.

*———. "A Spiritualist's Laryngitis Has Spirits Rasping." *Chicago Daily Tribune*, August 8, 1945.

*———. "Voodoo School Spirit Wooers Pour on the Oil." *Chicago Daily Tribune*, August 7, 1945.

Wolf, Tony. "Houdini: How Rose Mackenberg Took on Phantoms and Fakes." *Atlas Obscura*, May 5, 2016.

Worden, Helen. "Exposing Tricks of the Fake Mediums." *Popular Science*, Vol. 145 (November 1944): 67–71, 213–14.

Young, James C. "Magic and Mediums." *New York Times*, May 7, 1922.

Young, Jeremy C. "Empowering Passivity: Women Spiritualists, Houdini, and the 1926 Fortune Telling Hearing." *Journal of Social History*, Vol. 48 (Winter 2014): 341-62.

## ADDITIONAL INFORMATION FROM THESE SOURCES:

*Americus* [GA] *Times-Recorder*
*Atlanta Constitution*
*The Atlantic*
*Austin* [TX] *American*
*Austin* [TX] *Statesman*

*Baltimore Sun*
BBC.com
*Birmingham* [AL] *News*
*Boston Globe*

Brooklyn [NY] *Daily Eagle*
Brooklyn [NY] *Daily Times*
Buffalo [NY] *Sunday Times*
Burlington [IA] *Gazette*
*Business Insider*

*The Chat* [Brooklyn, NY]
*Chicago Daily Tribune*
*Cleveland Morning Leader*
*Commercial Appeal* [Memphis, TN]

*Daily News* [New York, NY]
*Davenport* [IA] *Gazette*
*Deseret News* [Salt Lake City, UT]

Elmira [NY] *Star-Gazette*
*Evening Independent* [St. Petersburg, FL]
*Evening Star* [Washington, DC]
*Evening Sun* [New York, NY]

Galveston [TX] *Daily News*
Garnett [KS] *Journal-Plaindealer*
*GQ*
*The Guardian*

Hanford [CA] *Sentinel*
*Harper's Weekly*
*Herald of Progress* [New York, NY]

*Indiana State Sentinel*
intervalmagic.com/houdini

*Journal of American History*

*Kennebec Journal* [Augusta, ME]

Lancaster [PA] *New Era*
Lancaster [PA] *Sunday News*
Lansing [MI] *State Journal*
LilyDaleAssembly.org

MeasuringWorth.com
*Minnesota Pioneer*
*Morning News*

*New Scientists*
*New-York Daily Tribune*
*The New Yorker*
*New York Evening World*
*New York Herald Tribune*
*New York Times*
*New York World*

Oakland [CA] *Tribune*
Omaha [NE] *Daily Bee*

Pittsburgh [PA] *Sun-Telegraph*
*Post-Press* [El Centro, CA]
*The Province* [Vancouver, British Columbia, Canada]
*Psychic News*

Richmond [IN] *Item*
Richmond [IN] *Palladium*

San Angelo [TX] *Evening Standard*
*San Francisco Examiner*
*Scientific American*
*Scribner's Magazine*
Seward [AK] *Daily Gateway*
*The Skeptic*
*Skeptical Inquirer*
*Smithsonian* magazine
*St. Louis Post-Dispatch*
St. Petersburg [FL] *Times*
*Suggestion* (magazine)
Sunday [NY] *Dispatch*

*The Times* [Shreveport, LA]
Tyler [TX] *Morning Telegraph*

Washington [DC] *Post*
Washington [DC] *Times*
*Weekly Pioneer and Democrat* [Saint Paul, MN],
*Weird Tales* (magazine)
WildAboutHoudini.com
Wilkes-Barre [PA] *Times Leader*
Winnipeg [Manitoba, Canada] *Tribune*

# INDEX

Page numbers in **boldface** refer to images and/or captions.

# PICTURE CREDITS

**George Britt**. "Houdini Traps Master Medium." *Burlington* [IA] *Gazette*, December 26, 1925: 93 (top and bottom).

"Keeping Up with the World." ***Collier's***, December 31, 1949: 118.

*Davenport* [IA] ***Gazette***, August 15, 1850: 18 (top).

*Evening Star* [DC], August 28, 1924: 82.

*Evening World* [NY], October 27, 1888: 48 (top).

**Flickr**, National Archives UK: 9; Lincoln Financial Foundation Collection: 35 (left); 62.

**Julia E. Garrett**. *Mediums Unmasked: An Exposé of Modern Spiritualism*. Los Angeles: H. M. Lee & Brothers, 1892: 48 (bottom left).

Courtesy of **Getty's Open Content Program**: 138.

*Harper's Weekly*, May 8, 1869: 34 (right).

**Harry Houdini**. *The Unmasking of Robert-Houdin*. New York: Publishers Printing, 1908: 26.

**Houdini**. *Houdini Exposes the Tricks Used by the Boston Medium "Margery," to Win the $2500 Prize Offered by the* Scientific American. New York: Adams Press, 1924: 80, 81 (bottom).

**Houdini**. "How I Do My 'Spirit Tricks.'" *Popular Science Monthly*, December 1925: 69.

**Houdini**. "How I Unmask the Spirit Fakers." *Popular Science Monthly*, November 1925: 89.

**Houdini**. *A Magician Among the Spirits*. New York: Harper & Brothers, 1924: 37, 40 (top), 61, 67, 98 (top).

**Houdini Collection**, in Joseph Dunninger. *Houdini's Spirit Exposés from Houdini's Own Manuscripts, Recordings, and Photographs*. New York: Experimenter Publishing, 1928: 20.

**Infinite Photographs**: 58 (top), 66.

**iStock**: GeorgePeters: cover; insjoy: 1; Sylfida: 2-3; sdominick: 4.

Private collection, **Gail Jarrow**: 39 (bottom), 137.

*Kennebec Journal* [Augusta, ME], November 1, 1926: 111 (top).

**Library of Congress, Prints & Photographs Division**, Lot 7441-H: 32, 45; LC-DIG ppmsca-36412: 58 (bottom); LC-USZ62-99116: 79; LC-USZ62-98931: 83 (left); LC-USZ62-122448: 83 (right); LC-USZ62-26516: 98 (bottom); LC-USZC4-1845: 140. American Red Cross Photograph Collection: LC-DIG-ds-01290: 60. Bain Collection: LC-DIG-ggbain-35697: 63 (right). Cabinet of American Illustration Collection: Yohn, no. 105: 40 (bottom). Farm Security Administration/Office of War Information Black-and-White Negatives Collection: LC-USF33-031074-M1: 121. Houdini Collection: LC-USZ62-112378: 24. Magic Poster Collection: LC-USZC4-5921: 33. McManus-Young Collection: LC-USZ62-96794: 21; LC-USZC2-6429: 23; LC-USZ62-112384: 25; LC-USZ62-112405: 50; LC-USZ6-2100: 53; LC-USZ6-2098: 54 (bottom); LC-USZ62-112419: 55; LC-USZ62-112434: 57 (right); LC-USZ62-112427: 72; LC-USZ62-112391: 77 (top left); LC-USZ62-112375: 77 (top right); LC-USZ62-112381: 77 (bottom); LC-USZ62-99115: 78; LC-USZ62-96051: 81 (top); LC-USZ62-66388: 87 (bottom);

LC-USZ62-112425: 88; LC-USZ62-112377: 104; LC-USZ62-112441: 112; LC-USZ62-112431: 114; LC-USZ62-96050: 129 (top); LC-USZ62-112420: 145. National Photo Company Collection: LC-DIG-npcc-27425: 100 (top); LC-DIG-npcc-27498: 103; LC-USZ62-111915: 105 (bottom); LC-DIG-npcc-03754: 106. New York World-Telegram and the Sun Newspaper Photograph Collection, LC-DIG-ppmsca-23994: 113. Performing Arts Posters Collection: LC-USZC2-1505: 56; LC-USZC4-709: 108. Rare Book and Special Collections: 2018682513: 107. Witteman Collection: LC-USZ62-79458: 11.

Rose Mackenberg. "Dwarf Inside 'Psychic' Drum Causes Expose of Myra's Mesmeric Music." *Winnipeg* [Manitoba, Canada] *Evening Tribune*, Magazine Section, March 16, 1929: 91.

Rose Mackenberg. "Mystic Cameras Dupe Bereaved with Fascinating Facts About Ectoplasm." *Winnipeg* [Manitoba, Canada] *Tribune*, Magazine Section, March 2, 1929: 90.

Rose Mackenberg. "Spiritualism, Possibly True, and 'Spiritualism' Demonstrably False." *Winnipeg* [Manitoba, Canada] *Evening Tribune*, Magazine Section, February 23, 1929: 96.

Rose Mackenberg. "When Crime Poses as Spiritualism." *American Weekly,* March 12, 1939: 95, 116, 117 (top and bottom).

William Marriott. "On the Edge of the Unknown: Physical Phenomena." *Pearson's Magazine*, Vol. 29 (June 1910): 74–75.

J. N. Maskelyne. *Modern Spiritualism: A Short Account of Its Rise and Progress, with Some Exposures of So-Called Spirit Media.* London: Frederick Warne, 1876: 28 (bottom left and right).

A. Medium. *Revelations of a Spirit Medium: or Spiritualistic Mysteries Exposed.* St. Paul, MN: Farrington & Co., 1891: 48 (bottom right).

*Minnesota Pioneer,* August 22, 1850: 18 (bottom).

William H. Mumler, "Mrs. Tinkham," The J. Paul Getty Museum, Los Angeles: 34 (left).

Carl Murchison, ed. *The Case For and Against Psychical Belief.* Worcester, MA: Clark University, 1927: 84.

National Library of Medicine, Images from the History of Medicine: A07262: 59.

*New-York Daily Tribune*, December 30, 1856: 15 (top).

Baron Von Schrenck Notzing. *Phenomena of Materialisation: A Contribution to the Investigation of Mediumistic Teleplastics.* London: Kegan Paul, Trench, Trubner, 1923: 64, 65.

Pacific Island Art Store: 57 (left).

Sidney Paget, illustrator. A. Conan Doyle. *The Memoirs of Sherlock Holmes.* London: George Newnes, Ltd, 1894: 63 (left).

Pexels: Photo by Aidan Roof: 129 (bottom); Photo by cottonbro studio: 133; Photo by Pavel Danilyuk: 136.

Harry Ransom Center, University of Texas at Austin: 28 (top right).

*Richmond* [IN] *Item*, February 17, 1926: 100 (bottom).

*Richmond* [IN] *Palladium*, February 20, 1850: 18 (middle).

*San Angelo* [TX] *Evening Standard,* November 1, 1926: 111 (bottom right).

*Saturday Evening Post Society*, licensed by Curtis Licensing, Indianapolis, IN. All rights reserved: 124, 125.

*Seward* [AK] *Daily Gateway,* November 1, 1926: 111 (bottom left).

**State Library of Victoria, Australia**, W. G. Alma Conjuring Collection: 28 (top left).

*Suggestion* **magazine**, October 1, 1901: 68.

Courtesy of the Special Collections Research Center, **Temple University Libraries**, Philadelphia, PA: 119, 122.

*Washington* [DC] *Times*, May 18, 1926: 105 (top).

**Lionel A. Weatherly, and J. N. Maskelyne**. *The Supernatural?* Bristol and London: J. W. Arrowsmith, 1891: 35 (right top), 42.

*Weekly Pioneer and Democrat* [Saint Paul, MN], June 12, 1863: 30.

*Weird Tales,* April 1924: 87 (top).

**Wikimedia Commons**, Missouri Historical Society, St. Louis: 12; Camp Chesterfield: 15 (bottom); 35 (right bottom); 39 (top); Theatrical Portrait Photographs, Harvard Theatre Collection, Houghton Library, Harvard University: 54 (top); 101; 126; 155.

# OTHER SPOOKY TITLES ABOUT MAGIC AND HOAXES BY GAIL JARROW

### The Amazing Harry Kellar: Great American Magician

Best Children's Books—Kirkus Reviews
Bank Street Best Children's Books
Nonfiction Honor List, VOYA
Nominee for the YALSA Award for Excellence in Nonfiction for
    Young Adults
TriState Young Adult Books of Note

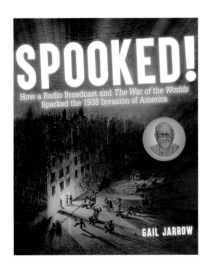

### Spooked! How a Radio Broadcast and The War of the Worlds Sparked the 1938 Invasion of America

Robert F. Sibert Award Honor Book—Association for Library
    Service to Children / American Library Association
Golden Kite Honor, Nonfiction for Older Readers—Society of
    Children's Book Writers and Illustrators
Notable Children's Book—Association for Library Service to
    Children (ALSC/ALA)
Notable Social Studies Trade Book for Young Readers—National
    Council for the Social Studies and Children's Book Council
Nominee for the YALSA Award for Excellence in Nonfiction for
    Young Adults
Quick Picks for Reluctant Young Adult Readers—Young Adult
    Library Services Association
Editors' Choice List—Booklist
Best Book—School Library Journal
Blue Ribbons List for Nonfiction—Bulletin of the Center for
    Children's Books
CCBC Choices Best of the Year—Cooperative Children's Book
    Center
Best Children's Book of the Year—Bank Street College of
    Education

# THE DEADLY DISEASES TRILOGY BY GAIL JARROW

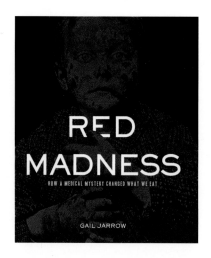

## Red Madness: *How a Medical Mystery Changed What We Eat*

Jefferson Cup for Older Readers—Virginia Library Association
Best Book—School Library Journal
Best STEM Book—National Science Teaching Association and
   the Children's Book Council
Best Children's Book of the Year, Science—Bank Street College
   of Education
CCBC Choice—Cooperative Children's Book Center

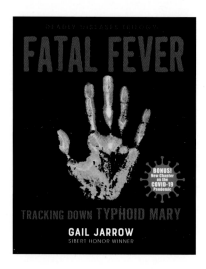

## Fatal Fever: *Tracking Down Typhoid Mary*

Eureka! Gold Award—California Reading Association
Blue Ribbons List for Nonfiction—Bulletin of the Center for
   Children's Books
CCBC Choice—Cooperative Children's Book Center
Best Children's Book of the Year, Outstanding Merit—Bank
   Street College of Education
Nonfiction Honor List—VOYA

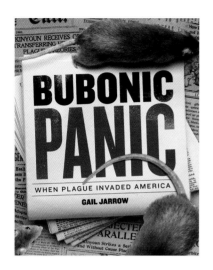

### *Bubonic Panic:* **When Plague Invaded America**

Best Book—School Library Journal
Best Book for Teens/Best Teen Mysteries and Thrillers—Kirkus
    Reviews
Eureka! Gold Award—California Reading Association
Outstanding Science Trade Book for Students—National Science
    Teaching Association and the Children's Book Council
Recommended, National Science Teaching Association
Notable Social Studies Trade Book—National Council for the
    Social Studies and Children's Book Council
CCBC Choice—Cooperative Children's Book Center
Best Books for Teens—New York Public Library

# THE MEDICAL FIASCOES SERIES BY GAIL JARROW

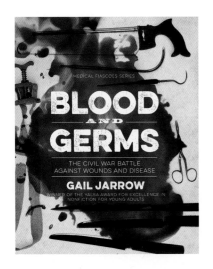

***Blood & Germs:*** *The Civil War Battle Against Wounds and Disease*

Kirkus Reviews Best Book (Middle-Grade Nonfiction)
Outstanding Science Trade Book for Students K–12—National Science Teaching Association and Children's Book Council
CCBC Choice—Cooperative Children's Book Center
Orbis Pictus Recommended Book—National Council of Teachers of English
Best Informational Book for Older Readers—Chicago Public Library
Charlotte Award, New York State Reading Association

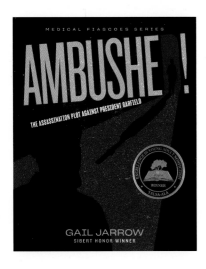

***Ambushed!*** *The Assassination Plot Against President Garfield*

Winner of the YALSA Award for Excellence in Nonfiction for Young Adults
Kirkus Reviews Best Book (Middle-Grade History)
CCBC Choice—Cooperative Children's Book Center
Grateful American Book Prize Honorable Mention

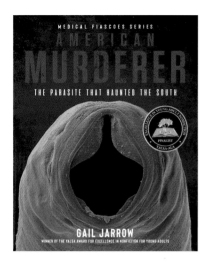

### American Murderer: *The Parasite That Haunted the South*

Finalist for the YALSA Award for Excellence in Nonfiction for Young Adults

Notable Children's Book—Association for Library Service to Children (ALSC/ALA)

Best Nonfiction Book—School Library Journal

Outstanding Science Trade Book for Students K–12—National Science Teaching Association and Children's Book Council

Best STEM Book—National Science Teaching Association and the Children's Book Council

CCBC Choice—Cooperative Children's Book Center

Best Informational Book for Older Readers—Chicago Public Library

# ALSO BY GAIL JARROW

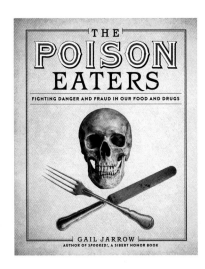

**The Poison Eaters: *Fighting Danger and Fraud in Our Food and Drugs***

Orbis Pictus Award for Outstanding Nonfiction for Children Honor Book—National Council of Teachers of English
Notable Children's Book—Association for Library Service to Children (ALSC/ALA)
Outstanding Science Trade Book for Students—National Science Teaching Association and Children's Book Council
Notable Social Studies Trade Book for Young People—National Council for the Social Studies and Children's Book Council
Best Children's Book—Bank Street College of Education
Kirkus Reviews Best Book (Middle-Grade History)
Blue Ribbons List—Bulletin of the Center for Children's Books
Editors' Choice: Books for Youth—Booklist
Lasting Connections, Top 30—Book Links
Best Children's Book—Washington Post

**GAIL JARROW** is the author of nonfiction books about magicians, misinformation and hoaxes, medical fiascoes, and other intriguing stories from American history. Her work has received many distinctions, including the YALSA Award for Excellence in Nonfiction for Young Adults for *Ambushed!*; the YALSA Excellence in Nonfiction Finalist for *American Murderer*; the Sibert Honor Book medal for *Spooked!*; the Orbis Pictus Honor Book for *The Poison Eaters*; an NSTA Best STEM Book and Outstanding Science Trade Book; an ILA Best Science Book; and the Children's Book Guild Nonfiction Award. She has a degree in zoology and has taught science to young students of all ages. She lives in Ithaca, New York. Visit gailjarrow.com.